# The Roma Chronicles

## By Bob Hitching

### Volume 1

### Jasmina, Darko and Milena

Spear Books
& Media

**Spear Books
& Media**

Spear Books
P.O. Box 330, Sevenoaks, TN13 1GF
England

ISBN 978-0956-01-9035
All Rights Reserved
© Robert Ian Hitching Budapest 2009

Neither this book nor any part may be reproduced or transmitted in any form or by any means, electronic or mechanical, including photocopying, microfilming, and recording, or by any information storage or retrieval system, without prior permission in writing from the publisher.
The consent of Spear Books does not extend to copying for general distribution, for promotion, for creating new works, or for resale. Specific permission must be obtained in writing from Spear Books for such copying.

Cover: copyright © Biblioteka Maleni, www.bibliotekamaleni.hr
Designed by: Nolda studio, www.noldastudio.com

Printing and Binding Lightning Source UK Ltd.
Chapter House
Pitfield
Kiln Farm
Milton Keynes
MK11 3LW

# Acknowledgments

My thanks to a wide group of people who receive our weekly Roma Diary who acted as a focus group. Their input and suggestions on the manuscript have been invaluable. Special thanks to Ernest Abbott, Jim and Bonnie Ehlert, Paige Tighe, and Anne Clark for their suggestions to make the manuscript readable to our American and English friends.

Special thanks to my daughter Galina for input and advice on the aesthetics involved in providing for the modern reader.

Special thanks also to Angie Cole for transcription and to Barbara Kornis for proofing and edting.

Special thanks to my Croatian Publishers and dear friends Zoran and Marija Jelic at Maleni Publishing for permission to use the cover from the Croatian edition.

Special thanks once more to my friend and English language publisher Roger Malstead at Spear Books for taking yet another risk on something I have written that does not fit the usual mold.

# Dedication

To my beloved wife, Dear Nancy, you are my best friend, my counselor and soul mate. Only you know how real this story actually is.

# Introduction

The story of the Balkans is a complex one. For generations the various ethnic groups in this part of the world have lived in a tension that on many occasions has spilled over into violence that seems to belong more to the Middle Eastern wars of the first millennium rather than in the modern epoch.

Yugoslavia began to break up officially in the 1990's, which led to a domino effect of regional wars in the former territories. Simplistic analysis made it easy to blame the Serbian side in the conflict. The Serbs were guilty but not as mindless marauding mad men driven by the intoxication of nationalistic superiority. In reality the issues are far more complex with hidden layers of symbols with their meanings and memories that stretch back to the second world war and much earlier where the most violent forms of religious nationalism seemed to drug otherwise reasonable neighbors. Standing back and watching the last 100 years it is very hard to identify who is innocent and who is guilty. One thing is for sure and that is that all parties claim innocence with religious fervor.

The breath-taking, bestial brutality that has clothed Catholic, Orthodox and Muslim actions, is of a nature that would be considered extreme in any time of history. Extreme not just in its paroxysms of hatred but also in its inability to ever see itself as guilty. Catholic, Orthodox and Muslim defend their actions with anecdotes of atrocities that the "other side" or "they" have committed. It is as if being a recipient of pain or injustice, by default releases one from any responsibility for ones own acts of injustice and violence. Herein lies the great ambiguity and heart wrenching reality of this region of the world.

In the midst of this highly complicated social construction are the Roma or Gypsies. They have been brutalized by all the parties and yet have been innocent of any crime when it comes to mass rape, genocidal murder and the wide spread destruction of property. Yet, the one issue that binds the otherwise warring parties of Catholics, Orthodox and Muslims is their deep and bitter hatred of the Roma. The Roma are the European pariah class and the new demons of the Balkans.

To the onlooker from the outside it defies our imagination that a people can be so vilified as the modern day Roma in the Balkans. There is no country in Central and Eastern Europe where the Roma are not prejudged, oppressed and treated ill. Some would argue without being too general that the Roma so often put their worst foot forward in social settings. This may be true but there is no excuse for the systemic prejudice that has become an open sore within modern European society.

Only time will reveal the ramifications of this reality as slowly the Roma begin to collectivize and become a political power block.
      The three short novels that have been condensed into this Chronicle are fiction and yet true to life. In their pages I have tried to capture the life of the Roma. The narrative is true to life in that almost every scenario that appears in the following pages is based upon either eyewitness accounts or from my own experience. If you are not familiar with this part of the world you will be tempted to read what follows with a sense that it is drama to the extreme and that it is simply too fantastic to be true to life. You would be forgiven for thinking this. Sadly, it would not be the truth as the chaos and drama of this part of the world is a daily reality. No other group embodies this drama more than the Roma and it is their voice I pray will be heard.

*The Roma Chronicles* ─────────

*Jasmina, Darko and Milena*

Part One

Jasmina

The Power of Love

# 1
## The Smell of Death

The smell of her own body induced a wave of nausea. Her face, beaten and bruised, had been pushed into the soft dark earth and she could taste its grit as well as the blood in her mouth. Her teeth had been smashed against her lips and her nose broken by the fist of her unknown assailant. The stranger who by invading her most private space, had defiled the purity that she had so carefully preserved, to be one day, a gift for a husband.

Just behind her she could hear the soft, gentle sound of the small stream. How she wished she could slip into its fresh crystal flowing and wash herself clean. She paused in her thinking. How she wished she could crawl to it and drown herself.

Her clothes were torn to shreds and she lay limp as a rag doll attacked by the family dog and tossed discarded into a corner of the room. Her swollen right eye was completely shut and blood streamed from her forehead. Her attacker's final act of brutality had been to take his knife and carve the sign of the cross on her tender flesh so 'sanctifying' his evil deed.

From her left eye she could see her home. Her body racked with pain, she observed the door behind which there had once been laughter and music, a father who adored her, a mother who, though conservative, saw her as a friend as much as a daughter, her beautiful sister and her dear little brother, Hamid, whom she regarded almost as a son rather than a sibling. Only silence issued from the little house now. It seemed as though hell lay behind the once friendly door.

## Jasmina, Darko and Milena

In the distance she could hear the screams of other young women whose lives were being ruined forever. Mingling with their desperate cries for mercy was a mixture of laughter and mockery.

The world was coming to an end. She knew she was about to die one way or another. If she mustered the strength to lift her body and thus show signs of life, she would only be treated once more as an object without value other than as a plaything for evil men, or she would be shot like a wild dog. If she lay there much longer she would simply die, for the will to live had left her.

On the fence just a few feet away sat a white dove, its fragile form a contrast to the madness of rape and murder that filled the air. She looked at its purity and longed to be able to transform herself into such a creature and fly away. She wanted to cry but only an agonizing whine passed from her soul, through her lips onto the bloodstained soil. She tried to speak, but no words emerged, so she thought them as she looked towards the beautiful bird. "Please fly away before they come and hurt you."

The sky was beginning to darken, the mysterious curtain of dusk was descending as if creation itself was embarrassed at such scenes of suffering.

Suddenly, she became aware of someone standing next to her. She closed her eyes and sought to move inside herself. There was a crack in the soil and she imagined herself forcing her spirit to leave her body and move into the earth, to feel the safety of its enclosure pressing her body into a mold where she could exist until all this was over. Thoughts raced through her mind, adrenalin heightening the moment and fueling the mental activity. She imagined she could hear her father and see his face. He was crying but the sound transposed into that of the bird cooing in the background. The vision changed to thoughts of hope that perhaps she had merely been beaten not violated and all would heal in a few days. These vestiges of hope were followed in their turn by unspeakable confusion and sordid pictures in her mind. She could feel herself pushing her soul further into the crack in the ground. She tried to stop breathing, to force herself to die, but her lungs disobeyed, gulping instinctively for air against her will.

She was startled, the face of her consciousness slapped, as she felt a hand touch her shoulder. She recoiled even further into herself imagining the crack in the ground growing into a great vortex of swirling energy. She found herself wishing that she were a diseased prostitute so that this defiler would be robbed of his joy in corrupting her innocence. Her mind was spinning. For a brief moment she experienced a flash of anger, an anger with a healing quality to it that drew her jumbled thoughts together. She opened her eyes, ready to curse with a string of words heard as a child from an aunt who dealt in such things.

Her eyes met those of a young boy about 12 years old. She gasped, " Stefan, Stefan Petrovic." Stefan Petrovic was generally referred to as the village idiot. He never spoke nor, for that matter, communicated at all. He would hang around the little Orthodox Church in the village. To some of the Roma Muslims he was an object of scorn and stories too crude to repeat were circulated about him. To some of the Christians he was an object of mockery, to others someone to be petted and indulged.

Jasmina had always had a warm place in her heart for him. He was a gentle boy and his father and mother were good people, forever trying to foster a sense of unity between the Roma Muslims and Christians in the village.

Stefan looked down at her. Instinctively she wanted to cover herself. The boy turned and stumbled towards her home.
The door felt too heavy as if it held an abnormal weight. He pushed hard and it swung slowly open. His gaze fell, horrified, on Jasmina's sister tied to the kitchen table her throat slit and her eyes cold with a glassy stare. He tried to turn away but found himself transfixed by

her lifeless body. He wanted to run to the church and crawl into one of the corners. In his mind he could smell the incense that made him feel secure without knowing why.

He walked into the next room to find Jasmina's little brother lying dead on the floor, his eyes mutilated. His outstretched hand grasped the hand of his dead father whose body was riddled with bullets. Who had reached out to whom? He wondered to himself.

Stefan grabbed a shawl, a scarf and coat and turned to go back to Jasmina. As he re-entered the first room he stopped and gasped. He saw now why the door, the heavy door by which he had entered, was swinging awkwardly. The crucified form of Jasmina's mother was nailed to it. His young mind swam and he began making sounds of grief, as he stumbled out into the garden where his young friend lay. He knelt down and vomited on the ground.

Jasmina, who was moving in and out of consciousness, came around. The feeling of warm clothes covering her body gave a sense of comfort. Stefan gently placed the scarf around her head and with great care pulled the material forward to cover the bloodstained sign of the cross. She tried to move but could not. Her legs seemed numb from the waist down and her back and neck were pounding as if someone was kneading dough on a stone slab. She felt the gentle touch of warm tears trickling from her eyes onto her bloodied cheeks. The tears drew lines in the dry caked blood on her face. Their journey was like a river pushing its way to some undisclosed destination.

Stefan, finding energy beyond his natural strength, reached down and pulled her into a sitting position then hoisted her to her feet. At once she fainted from the pain. With her arms over his shoulders he dragged her along, making his way towards the woods. He could still see the bodies of his mother and father lying in the street. Not incense but smoke seemed to swirl around them. He showed no emotion.

## The Roma Chronicles

Slowly, he dragged Jasmina well into the forest, out of sight of the village. Placing her carefully on the ground he went to the stream and cupped water in his hands, first drinking it himself and then pouring more over her wounds. With his handkerchief he bathed her face washing away both the blood and the tracks of her tears.

The door swung open with such force that Ivan thought it would come off its hinges. His father, a tall man in his late forties, stood in front of him. The anger on his face was so intense that Ivan thought him to be in danger of a stroke. He spoke with raised voice. " When I say that I forbid you to go, that's final!" Ivan raised his hand to try to break the tension and offer some defense. He smiled placatingly with understanding but his father continued. " I hate the Serbs! They're scum sucking, foul, evil slugs, and I have little more love for those circumcised Gypsy thieves that you call Muslims. They're all possessed by demons, they're filth beyond words. Not one person in their whole tribe can be trusted."

Ivan jumped up, his smile turning to a flash of anger. He paused, looked at the floor and composed himself. " I know how you feel, but I'm going. They need my help as an administrator and that's that. This camp is a special one just for Muslims, nobody wants them but I am going to at least try and help. Just because you feel this way does not mean that …." His father raised his voice even more. " Don't argue with me! If you go, don't come back and don't think I'll change my mind, once I've made a decision that's final."

Ivan smiled, and found himself calming down as he did so, but he spoke as firmly as his father. " You will change your mind you always do. You're tough talking on the outside but inside you're soft."

" Don't talk to me like ….." Now it was Ivan's turn to take control. "What about the time that little gypsy girl kissed you on the cheek when you gave her some money? You nearly cried, right there in the street."

Ivan's father quieted down. " Well, that was different, but why do this to your mother? You know what these camps are like. It's so easy to get cheated or even worse. Let NATO take care of them. Your mother's in the other room crying and saying she'll die if you go."

Ivan looked across towards the door in the direction of where his mother was. He felt a sense of pain that he was hurting his parents yet he knew deep inside himself that he could not turn back now. " You know why I have to go." His father spoke softly now. " Well, when are you leaving? I'll drive you to the train station."

As he said this, Ivan's sister, Marija, entered. She was tall with long brown hair reaching to her waist. There was a softness about her face and a beauty to her deep brown eyes that came from experience and pain rather than from the cosmetics jar. She smiled but seemed slightly detached from the interchange going on. " Actually, I would like to take Ivan down to the station."

Ivan's father interjected one last time with an appeal for sanity and a stream of abuse for gypsies and Serbs, before reaching out to hug his son once more and quickly leaving the room.

Marija spoke. " He's like a child when his feelings are hurt he lashes out in anger." She smiled. " Just like you!"

Ivan stood up, reached out to his sister and held her in his arms. " You know why I have to do this, don't you?" She gently pulled away then patted his shoulder. " No I don't, not really, so many of our own people are in need. Why go to these Gypsies? They are so different. You will be a tourist down there."

He looked into her eyes. She knew more of this wretched war than most. Her husband of less than three months had been killed

and her grief at his death had resulted in the miscarriage of their child. She had depth of character, but sadness, a pervading sadness, hung over her.
" Well at least let's write to each other." She nodded as they both walked towards the door.

Four young men sat together in a circle around a tiny fire in the woods. Steam drifted from their clothing into the air as their damp forms were touched by the heat of the few small burning logs. Their guns and backpacks lay close to where each of them sat. They all chewed intently on the hunks of meat, which they held in their rough, dirty bare hands. The cold damp air was still and silent apart from the sounds of small animals. At first, few words were exchanged by the members of the group.

Nadji Ahmedovich looked at his comrades. " I've never eaten pork before, it's good." An oily grin from his nearest companion seemed to break the ice. " Well, what can I say, you bad Muslim. Pass me the wine!" All four burst out laughing.

They had come upon an empty Serb village, the inhabitants having left before vengeance could reach their borders. The young men had scoured through the houses until they discovered a vein of wealth in the form of a kitchen filled with food.

Nadji spoke again. " It's all rubbish, all of it, Christian Priests and Muslim Imams blessing their guns and sending off their holy warriors to reclaim something or other. You can eat this meat but not that and you can't drink alcohol, eat this food on these days but you can rape my sister. I tell you, religion is always the problem. We are better off without any religion. Believe what you want and if there is a God he'll understand. I mean, if there is a God you'd think he'd talk with us directly instead of through priests and make it clear who's right and who's wrong. Anyway, I want to go to America that's where I want to be. I'm going to pick up my wife and boy and just get out of here. They say anyone can get a job and a car and do whatever they please."

Nadji gazed into the fire's embers and began to look and feel deeply melancholic. There was a silence of knowing in the group. It was as if their feelings, the fire, the damp rising from their clothes, had all merged into a moment of stilled and quiet consciousness.

Nadji spoke once more in a sad, quiet yet deliberate voice.
" I think I'll start a new religion: get up in the morning and kill a Serb, go to work and then for lunch kill a Serb, then at the end of the day...."
Before he could finish one of the others held out a hunk of pork.
" Here have some Serb's leg!" Nadji burst out laughing and started gnawing on the forbidden flesh.

# 2
## Peace

The sun poured through the trees with such a sensation of light that Jasmina was roused from her sleep. The pain in every part of her body resulted in an almost total inability to move. As well as the physical pain she was now beginning to feel the mental and emotional pain of the experience replaying constantly in her mind.

She now wished that she could go back and relive the event but this time with a knife or a gun or something that she could use to protect herself. She now knew too, that her family must be dead. She sensed it even in Stefan's manner.

The horror of such a day dawning and destroying everything that one loved and held precious was almost impossible for her to cope with. She simply wanted to die, to die quietly and drift softly away to wherever one goes when one dies.

Stefan knelt beside her and looked at her face. She could see the cross dangling from a chain around his neck. It seemed to mock at her as it tumbled against his young chest. Intuitively, as he looked at the mark on her forehead he made the connection in his sensitive young heart. Undoing the clasp he removed the chain, holding it gently in his hands, stood up, walked a few meters and started to look around, and then spotting a tree with many nooks and crannies, he reached over and placed the cross in one of them.

Jasmina felt awkward. She wanted to tell him not to do it, that she understood, but no words would come. He knelt down beside her once more and continued his watch over her. In his own limited way he knew he must find food and water and some kind of medical

## Jasmina, Darko and Milena

help for his friend or she would simply die there in the forest.

A young man in his late twenties opened the door and ushered his companion into the room. Ivan could tell from his accent that he was from the Podravina.

" It is not very big, Zagreb, but it's all we have." Ivan was standing with this new colleague in a small office that doubled as a bedroom. He smiled at his new friend's manner of calling him Zagreb instead of by name.

He looked around at his new home. The room boasted one window, a desk and in the far corner a sink. There was a clinical feel to the place yet he felt grateful that he could be there and play a part in helping.

His colleague continued. "Food, Zagreb, is any time you want in the cafeteria. It's all UN humanitarian aid stuff. Watch out for the fruity rings cereal, it was one of those American non-profit dumping jobs, they couldn't use it in the west so we have it here."

Ivan laughed. " What do you mean?" His friend, whose tone was mischievously cynical, smiled. " It's the die, Zagreb, it's blue. They had it on the market in America then suddenly found that the blue loops gave the children blue pee when they went to the toilet. So true to capitalism, they sent three tons of blue pee producing cereal to the barbarians of Central Europe as humanitarian aid. So if you have blue pee, don't go to the doctor, just send a sample to Bill Clinton."

Ivan laughed again and walked over to his desk. " So I sit here and interview people and then decide whether they should go to America, Germany, Australia or be kept here?" Darko nodded. " Right, but remember, Zagreb, the ones with the blue pee have to go to America." His new friend left the room with a chuckle.

Ivan sat in the chair behind the desk and looked out of the

window. He could see row after row of portable wooden huts that were now temporary homes for people just like himself. These people who had once lived in and belonged to villages and towns but were now homeless, were, it seemed to him, just pawns in a very big game. He reached into his bag and began to unpack his few belongings and placed his Bible in the top drawer and a photograph of his parents and sister next to the small desk calendar. He put a small radio on the desk and fiddled with the tuning knob until he found something jazzy that he could lose his feelings in.

Marija sat at her own desk and began to write a short letter to her brother. The clock on the wall entreated her to wait until later as she was so tired and worn out emotionally from the day. She disobeyed the clock, settling into what was to be the pattern of her life, drifting into a troubled sleep just as the sun rose on a city that looked to it daily for renewal and hope. She held the pen, looked at the picture of her dead husband in front of her, reached down to her stomach to consider what might have been and then began her nightly vigil of tears.

Jasmina was suddenly shaken awake by the sound of four young men with guns surrounding her and Stefan. She sensed Stefan draw close to her seeking both to protect her and be protected by her presence. Nadji looked around and then crouched close to them. He looked steadily into Jasmina's face and then at Stefan.
" It's OK, you're safe, we're Muslims."
Jasmina neither moved nor spoke. Stefan remained rooted to the spot. She could tell from the speaker's accent that he was from central Bosnia.
Nadji looked with concern at this younger woman. He could

see at a glance what she had endured and knew what she had been put through. His anger was tempered only by compassion. His voice was soft as he spoke. " I need to know your names. We have ways of passing you through a line to get you out of here, but I need your names."

Jasmina looked at Stefan and thought rapidly. She could barely speak but in an audible whisper she replied, "Jasmina Bajrami, this is my brother Hamid, the rest of my family are dead."

Stefan looked at Jasmina and then at Nadji without speaking, her name gave her away. She was a Gypsy, a Muslim Gypsy. " Hamid cannot speak but he understands everything you say."

Nadji looked at the ground and then slowly stood up and walked a few feet away. Jasmina could hear him cursing and swearing to himself and the ground. He turned back to her. "One of us will go and get some medicine and some help to move you. We can give you food and blankets for now."

Jasmina could feel the tears starting, but buried her face in Stefan's, or rather 'Hamid's', lap.

Nadji took a blanket from his backpack and gently laid it over her broken body. She looked such a sweet and innocent girl. He thought about what her life would be like now. No one would marry her, she might even be pregnant and some of these clean Gypsy girls would not allow an abortion. Her own family would reject her, there was no hope for her. It would have been better if she had died. He swore again under his breath.

One of the others had made a fire and was cooking some meat. He motioned to Nadji to come over. " Tell them it's wild deer, you can't tell the difference, but they may not eat it if they know it's pork."

After what seemed a short period of time three people carrying a stretcher came into their newly built camp. The thought of any man touching her made Jasmina feel nauseous, so it was a great relief to see a muscular, intense looking woman in her thirties approaching with a needle.

    The lady smiled, speaking softly as she gently took Jasmina's arm and without asking permission gave her an injection. She could just remember hearing her say the words, "It's immediate," before a great rushing, whooshing feeling of peace and stillness flooded her consciousness. All the pain immediately ceased and she had no desire to move. The faces of the people around her seemed angelic. Great sobbing convulsions which, somehow added to the sense of peace, engulfed her. " Oh, my, my thank you." As they placed her on the stretcher she found herself reaching for Hamid's hand. Then as they lifted the stretcher the all-encompassing peace became a deep sleep.

# 3
## The Meeting

A feeling of early morning in spring wafted over Jasmina's emotions as she found herself slowly waking. She could hear her father laughing in the other room. The smell of coffee and fresh bread gave her a sense of safety and security. She could hear Hamid running up the outside stairs to the room on the side of the house. Her sister was arguing with her mother in the kitchen, and even this was so familiar that it made her feel safe. She laid still for a moment her eyes still closed.

Suddenly, without warning, the sounds disappeared and the smell of coffee and bread gave way to a damp stale odor that made her feel sick. Her eyes opened. She was lying on a bed in a small dirty room. She could now hear sounds of men talking and swearing. The language shocked her. She could tell from their accents that they were Muslims.

She tried to move her body but the pain resisted her efforts. There was a shaft of light that came through a large crack in the wall. She closed her eyes again, as she sensed the presence of someone coming into the room.

The same woman who had given her the injection in the field was now sitting beside her. Jasmina looked at her and then spoke softly. " I thought I was at home and that none of this had happened."

The woman who looked so strong nodded. " That would be from the drugs we gave you, it may still come and go, they are very strong. You are badly injured. I need to give you some more medication now."

Jasmina lay still. The woman continued to speak. " If you are pregnant we can get rid of it for you, but you will have to make the decision."

There was no feeling in Jasmina's heart as the words were spoken. " When can you tell if I am or not?" " It is going to be a while but you can't leave here yet anyway, you are too sick to travel. I'll be coming and going and will take care of you."

The woman took Jasmina's arm and gave her another injection. Jasmina looked at the wall and gently nodded her thanks. She found herself drifting again and now it seemed as though she could see her father walking towards the house with a newspaper under his arm. He was smiling.


Marija stood looking down into the river. The towering blocks of flats south of her seemed so impersonal in a place that used to be known for its sense of community. She watched the deep waters moving with such majesty beneath her. She thought and wondered what it would be like to jump in. She found herself almost gasping for breath as in her mind she saw herself sinking beneath the waters. It caused her soul to shudder.

Life made absolutely no sense at all. Yet death was something she found herself recoiling from. She was, like so many, engulfed by a sense of disappointment so strong as to be almost physical. It was an inner boredom and tiredness wrapped up in a feeling of subdued anger.

She could see herself as a little child with her family walking up to the old city. The big iron chain that is still there, and seemed always to be there, hooked to the old wall, beckoned her back to childhood to sit upon it's ancient form.

She could almost see the reflection of her husband in the

water. He had been such a good man. He had loved her and talked with her so much. He had listened with understanding. He had helped her make sense of life by their own companionship. She could almost feel her lips burn with the memory of their first kiss. She had felt weak and warm, safe and yet excited.

Then, in her mind's eye, she saw the door open with the two soldiers standing there asking to come in and telling her to sit down. The words that he had been killed seemed to come from afar like as if in an echo chamber. She reached into her purse and took a cigarette. The lights coming from the buildings gave an almost unwelcome comfort. For a moment she thought to herself that there needed to be music.

The door opened. The cold winter air rushed in, expelling in a moment the heat that had taken nearly half an hour to generate. " Zagreb, I have got a bad one for you, been here a week but they were weeks up river, remember to ask if their pee is blue." Ivan raised his hand dismissively, brushing his friend aside.

He looked up to see Jasmina and Hamid standing before him. He smiled and motioned for them to sit down. Jasmina was dressed in a gray sweatshirt. She also wore baggy jeans and sneakers and an awkwardly fitting scarf covering her forehead. Her face showed traces of recovery from a bad beating, Her lips still revealed the marks of recently removed stitches. Next to her stood Hamid, dressed in similar clothes that did not fit. They both sat down, Jasmina looking permanently at the floor.

Ivan spoke, but began praying inwardly. " I have to fill out some forms and then we'll try to get you placed as quickly as possible. I see you were able to get some clothes from Humanitarian. Sorry if it's not exactly Di Caprio. "

*The Roma Chronicles* ─────────

He expected a laugh in response to this, to break the tension, but none came. He had now seen and heard story after story of rape, torture, death and destruction. He had discovered that he had become hardened to these tales, not in a deliberately unfeeling way but as a defense mechanism, just as a workman's hands develop calluses so his own emotions had been at first raw and sore, then blistered, then hardened. Every so often, however, a case would penetrate his defenses and get through to him. Before he had heard even one word from the two sitting in front of him, he knew this was going to be one of those.

He looked at the young woman's face. There was a delicacy about it. Her lips formerly injured, were not richly crimson, but rather an almost pastel golden color. Her green eyes were soft and intense and the fall of the bright auburn hair with coppery tints escaping from beneath her scarf reminded him for some reason of the sails of ancient Moorish ships billowing in the wind on their trade routes between Morocco and Spain. Her form was innocently sensuous.

Little conversation was exchanged as Ivan filled out the forms in response to quickly answered questions. He asked them to return the following day when he hoped to have some information for them. Ivan handed her a sealed envelope. " This is from medical. I guess it is test results of some kind." Jasmina took the envelope, knowing what the tests were.

Jasmina and Hamid stood up together. As she turned to leave she looked at Ivan and for the first time their eyes met briefly. A rush of feeling seemed to pass between them, feeling that seemed to change into an almost physical flow of warmth, causing them both to feel uncomfortable. She quickly looked away, nodded and left.

Ivan sat down and looked out of the window as the pair walked slowly back to their rooms. There was so much sadness in this girl and her little unspeaking brother. What was it though, that was different about her? She reminded him of the sadness his sister displayed. He reached into the drawer and pulled out his Bible. He was just about to open it when a change of temperature in the room announced the arrival of his 'chief samples analyst'.

"Zagreb, what was…?" Ivan raised his hands together halting the question and answering at the same time. " Black with green spots."
" Zagreb, Zagreb, then you know what you must do, off to Pakistan with them!" Ivan immediately felt guilty that he had joked about someone who had suffered beyond his comprehension.

Nadji stood alone looking down at the dead bodies of his companions. He displayed no emotion. Standing with guns pointing at him stood three other men with long black beards and heavy looking crosses around their necks. One moved forward. He was tall and muscular and wore green and brown combat fatigues. He spoke to Nadji. " So, what do we do with you then? Shall we offer you a last meal before you die?"

Nadji turned and looked at him, this man whom he didn't know and yet hated so intensely. He could imagine him being one of those who had defiled that young Gypsy girl with the mute little brother.

He smiled and spoke. " No, thank you. It's OK we just ate. There was a Serb family just down the road." He pointed to his left. " Just over there… actually the mother looked a little like you, she had a similar beard, anyway after I killed them I roasted them, but you know the meat was a little….."
A single bullet was fired directly into his face before he could finish.

# The Roma Chronicles

Jasmina stood in the toilet cubicle next to her hut. She opened the envelope and pulled out a slip of paper. For a moment a sense of joy washed over her as she realized that she was not pregnant. She flushed the paper and envelope down the toilet. For a moment she stood still. Her mind became a flood of thoughts not so much about the past but rather the future. If she had been pregnant she would at least have had a child but now she would never marry and never know what it would be to nurse a child and be loved and love in return. A deep shudder gripped her heart at the thought.

Marija walked out into the street from the small Pizza place just down from Illica. The wind was brutal and she wrapped her long black wool scarf around herself, adding to the mass of clothing that she had already put on to ensure her survival as she ventured outside. She walked south and took the cable car up to the old city where she walked some more.

She would go to the stone gate and light a candle for her husband and child. Just doing something in memory of them was a proactive and healing action. She found herself humming the music to O Mio Babbino Caro, its melancholic strands connecting with the depth of sadness she was feeling.

After standing in silence for a while before the array of candles that had turned a mere gateway and a cobblestone street into a sacred place of memories, she retraced her steps in the direction of the main city. She felt within herself a deep sense of betrayal and alienation from God and the heavens in general.

The streets blurred as her pain mingled with the physical experience of walking through a neighborhood that had been unchanged for generations.

Turning into a pedestrian area she saw before her the Serbian Orthodox church. Without really knowing why she began to walk towards its western side. The tall gray building appeared to be standing there in defiance of her and her view of God. Her moist breath seemed to turn into the smoke of rage coming from the nostrils of one who cried for vengeance against injustice. She realized how quickly hatred could ascend from a soul in pain.

Without knowing how or why she ran across the small green area, picked up a stone and threw it at the building, cursing as loudly as she could. For a split second she felt a rush of euphoria. She was taking action.

The adrenalin intensified as a policeman running towards her shouted at her to stop. She turned, her long brown hair swirling as she bent over and picked up another stone and threw it again at the building that remained impassive.

Behind her she could hear a group of young people cheering as she reached into the most profane part of her consciousness to utter a string of words that would have shocked the most hardened of heart.

She bent again to pick up a third stone to hurl at the symbol of hypocrisy and injustice just as the policeman who had called out to her to stop seized her by the arm. She pounded his chest, crying out for the man she had loved and the baby who had been stolen from her.

Ivan closed the door to his room and walked out into the night air. It was cold but clear, one of those evenings with an air of freedom that seemed to cover the awful sadness contained behind the walls of these makeshift homes. He walked slowly down the pathways between the little wooden buildings, which radiated a heat that seemed to reach out and touch him.

He picked up a discarded tin can and tossed it aside. He could see Jasmina and Hamid standing in front of a doorway to one of the wooden buildings. His eyes sought to make contact with hers but this time she was on the defensive. She looked down, gave barely a brief nod and turned to the door.

    Hamid stood still and looked at Ivan. He smiled and then with two fingers in a puffing motion asked for a cigarette. Ivan shook his head. He wanted to say that a little boy like Hamid should not smoke, but the idea of lecturing on health hazards to a kid who had seen his family murdered and maybe witnessed the rape of his sister did not seem particularly appropriate. However, he realized that the young man wanted to hang out with him so he invited him to come along. He had picked up from the earlier interview that this lad could understand everything but could not speak and was 'simple'. It was the latter description that bothered Ivan, because Hamid had an innate streetwise air about him.

    They reached the office and Ivan told Hamid to wait. He returned holding a small 20-centimeter wooden pipe. Neither flute nor recorder it was something in between. He handed it to his new young friend.

    Hamid looked at Ivan, held the pipe in his hands and smiled. " Listen, Hamid, learn to play it. It doesn't matter how it sounds just try and make the notes connect to your feelings."

    Hamid smiled, saluted and left. He trundled off down the path. Ivan saw him disappearing into the wooden building and found himself looking for just a glimpse of Jasmina. Through the cold night air came a familiar sounding voice. " Zagreb, some beer and salami, let's partake as we plan the rebuilding of the world as a place of harmony and love where Muslims, Serbs, Croats and Gypsies live together as Tito would have had them….."

Marija sat at her writing table and began once more to write a letter to her brother.

## Jasmina, Darko and Milena

"Dearest, I think of you every day. I wish I could say that I pray for you but right now no prayers will come out. Maybe it's because I can find nothing to thank God for and prayer without thanks seems to me to be just whining. Anyway, I went tonight up to the old town and looked out over the city. The sight was very powerful and I began to think back to when we used to go up there as children. You were too short and I would lift you up on the wall holding you tightly in case you fell over."
She stopped as the memory sank in and began to cry.
" Why do bad things happen? Why does love set us up for joy, only for life to destroy it? It would be better not to know love than to experience it only to have it shattered and ripped away. Where is my husband now? My baby, did it exist? Does it exist now?"

She stood up and walked over to the wall that held a mirror and a shelf with a clutter of envelopes and knickknacks. She picked up a cigarette, lit it and slowly inhaled the smoke. Blowing smoke into the mirror she looked at her reflection. Would she ever know love again? Her body ached to hold a baby. Walking back to the writing desk she found herself weeping yet again.


Jasmina lay on her bed in the darkness. She touched her forehead, feeling the outline of the cross scar. She felt safe in this place but memories kept racing through her mind. She wrestled inwardly with ideas of right and wrong. Was she pure or impure? She knew what her culture would tell her. But why should she be considered impure? She had done no wrong. Yet how could she ever be married? Why would she ever want to marry? But she longed to be loved, to be a wife and to have children. For weeks she had thought about her family. The pain of their death was muted by the fact that she had not seen them die or after they were dead. In some ways it still seemed unreal. She cried alone every night. Sometimes she thought to herself that she was grieving as much for herself as she was for them. The thoughts would make her feel guilty.

    She found herself wanting to punish someone. At times she wondered if this had happened to her because she was evil. She was not like the other girls in the village. She was like her father in spirit. She was from the city locked inside a village body and culture.

    She thought of Ivan. He was somehow different. He was normal but there was something deeper about him. She thought of the day earlier when their eyes had met. It was confusing. She had liked the feeling but it was more than that, there was something clean about his eyes and the way that he looked at her.

# A Good Man

Marija walked back past the Orthodox Church where she had had the outburst some days earlier. It now seemed unbelievable to her that she had acted in that way. She knew hatred but there was something inside her that acknowledged that hatred could only damage her more than it would damage any object of her hatred. She thought to herself that she ought to apologize to someone for what she had done, but whenever the subject came up in conversation and she tried to talk about it, her listener invariably burst out laughing saying, "Let's go and do it together!"

She had therefore decided that she must go to her priest and talk it through. He was such a gentle man and so humble and for some time now he had been calling on his people to forgive. It was not a popular call. She hurried up the road, making her way to her church. The sky looked angry as if the clouds were ready to pour vengeance upon the city.

Jasmina looked up from the filing cabinet at Ivan, who was engrossed in talking with a young man and filling out forms. She had been observing him ever since he had given her this job as his office assistant. She was confused, she had heard of girls who had been raped and of how they had no desire to be near men. She felt like that too, but not about Ivan. There was an intrinsic cleanness about him that made her feel drawn to him rather than repelled by him. The counseling she had received had helped a little, but she still had nightmares and every so often if she were alone, such a sense of panic would sweep over her that she thought she would pass out.

Ivan looked over at her and smiled. He looked back at the forms and then again at Jasmina. She was beautiful there was no doubt about that. Also, she was far more urban than he had expected her to be and she seemed very much aware of what was going on. She said her knowledge had come from listening to the radio and reading books that her father brought home for her from the library.

He knew that he could not pursue a relationship with her. She was a Muslim and he was a Christian. Despite what was dished up by the media it was not possible for a Muslim and a Christian to be joined together if they took their religions seriously.

His musing was interrupted by Darko's entrance. " People, civilization as we have known it has come to an end, either that or another shipment from Toyland is here because the crowds are rioting in the streets, the Tsar is dead, food is short…" Ivan raised his hand. 'Darko, no more! Are you telling us that a new shipment just arrived?"

Before Darko could answer the young man whose forms Ivan was filling out rushed from the room, brushing past Darko in his haste. Darko looked on and with a dry smile, spoke. " And thus they went to water, blind to their fate." He closed the door leaving Jasmina and Ivan alone.  Ivan smiled at Jasmina. She seemed so sweet and fresh despite her terrible ordeal. He motioned to her to take a seat. " Shall we talk?"

She smiled and sat down, folding one leg over the other. Even this action and her body language seemed unusual to Ivan. There was simplicity there, but also a certain level of sophistication and class, he thought to himself.

" I was wondering, and I promise you this is not a trick question, but what do you believe about God and religion?" Without hesitation, she smiled and spoke with almost childlike enthusiasm. " Well, the truth is I have never thought as much about this as I have done recently, and for obvious reasons. This is how I think. In my religion, God is not personal. I mean, when we pray we are not sure if God hears those prayers and certainly I can't know whether God will answer those prayers. It's as if that's is not the important issue. It's is more based on the things that we or I am supposed to do rather than what I am on the inside."

Ivan placed his chin on his hands, which were resting on the desk. He was wearing a black T-shirt and a gray jacket.
" How does that affect you I mean when you pray?" She thought for a moment and then answered, " Well, again, I never thought about this until recently. But when I used to pray, especially in the evening, we have a time for prayer just after sundown, I would finish my prayers and then I would talk to God about things, not in a conversational way like us now, but I would say, 'I don't want to stay in the village,' and things like that."

The door opened and Darko came in again. There was something ambiguous about him for he seemed always to be pretending that life was not really happening and that we were all just observers of everything that was going on around. His semblance of intelligent humor was also difficult to read. He was obviously an intelligent person but for some reason wanted to keep that side of himself under a veil.

" Zagreb and Dr. Jasmina, dinner is served and today it is worthy of no delay." This call to a higher service broke up the conversation and they all made their way to the canteen.

## The Roma Chronicles

Marija sat at Father Pavich's desk. His room was filled with books and files. He was known as a reader and also as someone who was a little on the fringe for he had often met with Protestants in the city which made him seem a little too liberal for some.

He listened calmly and without interruption to Marija's story, her husband, the child and the anger and hatred she was feeling. When she had finished he sat quietly for a while, and then his eyes began to fill up. He paused, taking out his handkerchief and dabbing his eyes as he spoke. " Hatred is something like a cancer. You either cut it out or it ultimately takes over your whole being. But you cannot deny it exists, there is no question about that. But my advice to you is this, find a Serb, not a man or woman who is healthy and strong, but maybe an old lady, perhaps a widow, or an orphan and serve them. Do not feel it, just do it, serve them and you will find that in that one person you can heal your own hatred and then love will replace the cancer."

For a moment Marija sat speechless. It was too sacred a moment to sully with questions or objections. The sound of an old clock ticking in the room was the only thing she was aware of except the pounding of her heart.

Jasmina walked up to Ivan's office and looked in at the window. He was kneeling down with his Holy book resting on a little table in front of him. She could see that his eyes were closed and his lips were moving. He was obviously praying. She found it very moving to watch him yet felt guilty that she was prying into something so personal and private. He was a good man, she could feel it. He was a good man. Ivan moved from off of his knees back to sitting at his desk. He picked up a pad of paper and took a pen from the drawer in his desk.

*Jasmina, Darko and Milena*

Dear Father,
This will sound strange to you but I have just been praying and I realized something very serious. When I left to come to the camp here I left with a bad attitude towards you and very little concern for the feelings of both you and mother. I showed disrespect to you and I was wrong. I know you did not want me to come down here and it is difficult now because I am here and so involved helping people. I apologize for the way I spoke and I do honor you and I want to show respect to you.

He continued the letter with news about the camp and his new friends and then signed it and placed it an envelope put a stamp on it and then placed it in the mail tray. As he lay down on his bed he found himself praying, " Lord, you have made these structures of authority and without them we would all live in chaos and anarchy like these poor people here. Make my life something that has submission and goodness to it not rebellion and selfishness. Help me not to disobey you in these feelings I have for Jasmina."

His conscience seemed immediately to be cleared and he drifted into a dreamless calm sleep.

# 5
## Love

Looking out of her window Jasmina saw the signs that spring would soon be upon them. There was something in the air that breathed a sense of freshness into life itself even when that life offered no real reason for either hope or meaning.

The camp was not a bad place, although the rumors and the need to keep one's business very much to oneself was the principle objective of most days, besides finding something good to eat and some more clothes from the unending supply of humanitarian aid.

It was now several weeks since she and Hamid had started coming to Ivan's office. Things were beginning to fit together and it was looking more and more likely that they would be placed in Germany in a small Gypsy community there. She had shocked herself by the way in which she had begun gradually to open up in conversation to Ivan and even though there was a shyness that she wished she could overcome she felt that they were slowly becoming friends. He had promised to write to her wherever she was placed. The affection developing between them was like that of brother and sister, but Jasmina knew, however, that something deeper lay beneath the surface, something they could not fully identify or even admit to themselves.

She liked him very much, but how did he feel towards her? Did he just feel pity for her, and why did she allow herself even to think about it when she knew that no man would take her? Why would she even begin to think that they might have a life together? He seemed to be religious, but not strange. His Holy book was often on his desk, he spoke of prayer and his life was clean. The way he looked at her was different from the ordinary, everyday exchanges she had with the rest of the men in the camp. Even the other aid workers were like that but Ivan was different. She gently touched the scar on her forehead.

Ivan knelt by his bed with his Bible open. He would often pray and read at the same time, talking with God as a friend not a landlord or a judge. Tonight he was reading the story of how Jesus healed a woman who had suffered from a blood disease for many years. The religious leaders had no answer for why she was like that and no word of hope for her. Jesus was different. It was if he could feel all her pain. She wanted to marry, to have children, to love and be loved. She wanted all the things that any woman wants but her life was ruined by this disease. He began to cry. This was dear Jasmina. This was his new friend for whom he felt a love that he could not admit even to himself, let alone to her. She, too, was suffering. He remembered the day when her scarf had fallen from her forehead in the office and she was suddenly aware that he could see the scar of the cross. How she had blushed with embarrassment. She had seen his response and the tears forming in his eyes. This is why he wept. He began to cry even more as he read how Jesus reached out and touched her and how she was released and healed. He was saying to her, 'I want to heal you so that you can enjoy life, be loved and love in return. I want you to know the joy of holding a little baby in your arms.'

Ivan looked at the ceiling, nursing the Bible in his arms. " Jesus, Oh Jesus, heal Jasmina, not for me but for her and for you." He held the Bible tighter as if he were holding her. " I just want to love her Lord. I just want to make her life happy. I just want to give good things to her. But I know it's impossible. She's a Muslim, Oh

Jesus, help me, my heart is hurting so much. I just want to do the right thing."

He thought of the letter he had written to his father and how he had known that submission to authority was not weak but strong. Even now he could feel the sense of responsibility not to ignore the words of the Bible about being married to someone who did not believe in Jesus. He knew what was right but doing right caused him great pain in his heart.

Three more men with guns stood in the clearing where the young Muslim men had been shot. They walked over to one who had been shot in the face, obviously at point blank range. One of the men bent down beside him. " This one is still alive, but what a mess."

Nadji Ahemedovic was unconscious, the bullet that had passed through his face lodged in a tree behind him. Another of the men spoke. " Kismet, that is what it is. If he had been one-meter back his head would be in the tree. Let's see if we can save him."

# 6

## The Confession

The door opened and Jasmina stood framed in the doorway as Ivan sat at his desk. He tried to act and speak naturally but inwardly he felt as if his heart were exploding with both agony and joy.

" Where is Hamid? He tried to behave normally as he gestured for Jasmina to take a seat and leant against the desk in an attempt to steady himself. How he loved her! He knew it and was no use trying to hide the fact from himself any longer. Jasmina smiled and looked straight into Ivan's eyes. " He's practicing on the wooden pipe that you gave him."

Ivan smiled, and then looking at Jasmina found his eyes becoming moist and his face beginning to flush. In turn she felt the energy of the moment.

" Jasmina, I can't put it any other way. I am in love with you. I adore you and I want to do whatever will make you happy. I mean I want to care for you, love you and be your man… I mean, oh God, Jasmina, I am in love with you."

The air seemed to become a vibrant burst of color and finely tuned sounds. She could feel a rushing sensation all over her body as his words emerged so awkwardly yet with such purity. She gasped.

She stood up again, looking across at Ivan who moved awkwardly behind his desk. He sat down and put his head in his hands. He spoke again, " I'm sorry Jasmina, I should never… Oh Lord, I am sorry, please don't…."

Catching her breath, she whispered, " Ivan…" Then she

began to cry but spoke softly yet firmly through her tears. " I love you, too ."

Suddenly, there was a knock on the door and Darko entered without waiting for a reply. " Zagreb, another customer in the clinic, all messed up, no head, but somehow seems to be able to communicate, the good news is, he won't have to go to the dentist….."

He looked at them both, suddenly aware that he had interrupted a personal encounter between the two of them. " JoJ, Joj, "Well, OK, maybe later, anyway…."

Darko left again as fast as he had come in. Ivan stood up. He wanted to reach out and hold Jasmina's soft form in his arms. He wanted to pull her scarf back and gently kiss the scar on her forehead. He wanted to tell her she was a virgin in his sight and he loved her in a way that was pure.

" Oh dear, dear Jasmina, can we walk together later when things slow down and just talk things through?"

She nodded and moved towards the door, then paused, turning to look at this dear young man, so kind so loving and so clean. She gazed into his eyes. " Ivan, you are precious, special, so precious." The door closed and Ivan immediately fell to his knees.

" Oh Lord, I am sorry, I have done exactly the very opposite to what I meant. I should have not said a word and now I am in deep, Help me Lord, No matter what, I will do what you say."

# 7
## The Truth

The sounds of shouting and screaming were coming from outside one of the huts near Ivan's office. The noise erupted into his room as Darko opened the door. " Zagreb, as we say in the cornfields of the Podravina, when fertilizer is on your boots it is worthy to be a peasant, when fertilizer is on your face, better to be a proletarian. Well, old friend there is, I am afraid, a lot of fertilizer in the air today."

Ivan looked outside and saw Jasmina holding Hamid close while a group of women screamed at them both. He ran to the scene to intervene.

A Gypsy woman in her fifties was standing in front of the group of screaming women. Her finger was pointing at Hamid as she yelled at Jasmina. " You know it's true! I've only been here two days and as soon as I saw him I knew it was him. Prove it by letting us see if he's circumcised. And you, maybe you are with the Serbs! Maybe you enjoyed them."

Ivan pushed his way into the group and called for everyone to be quiet. He tried as hard as he could not to reveal that his heart was pounding for Jasmina and that he wanted to take her away from all this.

" OK, OK someone tell me what's going on." The spokeswoman raised her voice and pointed at Hamid again." This dog is a Serb! She's a liar. I'm from the next village to theirs. He's a Serb, I tell you."

Relief swept over Ivan. Either the woman was crazy or there had been some simple misunderstanding. He began to laugh, trying to diffuse the tension. " He's a Muslim. His name is Hamid, you are simply mistaken."

He looked at Jasmina and a cold chill ran through him as he realized that something was not right. He spoke again, keeping his voice normal with a huge effort. " Jasmina and Hamid come with me to the office and we will sort this out."

In the safety of the room, Jasmina began to cry. " I could not tell even you, they would have taken him away. Stefan saved my life in the village and took me to safety in the woods, he's about the same age as my brother, the one who's dead, well I think he's dead, and…."

Ivan put his hand gently on her shoulder. "It's OK, it's OK, I'm not angry, but you will need to tell me everything."

Before she could begin once more the story of torture, rape and murder and of how she had escaped with Stefan, the door opened again without a warning knock.

" Sorry, Zagreb, you know what is all over the place, and the Pope wants to see you right now." Ivan stood as if rooted to the spot, his feelings rushing in all directions.

" Darko, stay here with these two, and don't leave until I get back."

He rushed through the narrow alleyways to the main administration building and went straight to the unit director. The Pope, as he was affectionately known, was a clearheaded man with many years' experience both of running large projects and especially of conflict resolution. He greeted Ivan with an expression of resignation as he shook hands and asked him to sit down.

"It seems we have a problem, well, actually we have two problems." Ivan looked up warily, not quite knowing how to react. " Problem number one is we have an uncircumcised 'Muslim' who is really a Serbian village idiot and problem number two is his surrogate 'sister' is in fact, according to the whispers in the canteen, emotionally involved with a staff worker."

Ivan sat quietly, his mind racing. The Pope stood up, walked over to the window, and looked out. " Ivan, I have to keep this place clean. I cannot stop people being people but I have to be the disinfectant in this place or it will turn into a garbage tip. So just tell me everything."

Ivan looked down at the floor and at the unit director's shoes. " I didn't know about the boy… but yes, I am involved with the girl…." The camp director interrupted. " What does being involved mean?" " I am in love with her." He nodded without smiling. " Again, what does that mean?" Ivan looked red in the face and then spoke. " There is no relationship just strong feelings."

The Pope stood leaning against his desk. " Look, you are a good kid and you could make a career of this kind of work. With Slobo on the loose, this is one sector that will have full employment. Tell me how do you propose to solve this?"

Ivan looked up, surprised. The camp director spoke again. " You are a bit young but remember what your parents told you about Tito's self management? got it?" Ivan smiled. " I have thought of a plan. Let me take the boy back to Zagreb with me and my sister will care for him. We can just write him out on a ticket as if he were going to any other place. She can get the coupons for his food and so forth. I will then transfer to another camp, that will take care of the problem of my being emotionally involved with the girl."

The Pope smiled. " OK do it, and when she is ticketed out of here you can come back, I don't want to lose you in the long term."


Darko smiled as Ivan reappeared after his interview with the Pope. Jasmina sat as if turned to ice, motionless and silent. Ivan spoke softly to Darko. " Take the boy over to the canteen and get him something to eat, then collect up his belongings please.

Everything is set up with the Pope."

As the door closed on Darko and Hamid, Ivan found himself weeping softly as he reached out his hand to Jasmina.

" I'm so, so sorry, Jasmina. I am so sorry. I should have kept my feelings to myself."

Jasmina still sat confused and motionless as. Ivan spoke again.

" We have to do something drastic. I have persuaded the director to let me take the boy to Zagreb. He can stay with my sister. I'll call her now and explain everything. But I have to leave this camp, because my feelings for you are going to compromise the situation here."

Jasmina asked quietly, " What will happen? What will happen to Stefan, to me, to you?"

She wanted to cry out that it wasn't fair, she had suffered so much and now she was going to lose both her best friend and Stefan. Where was the justice in that? What was the point of the Holy book or any holy book sitting on the table? What was the point of talking about prayer? Life was just one blow after another. She wanted to tell Ivan again that she loved him and that she wanted to hold him as well as to be held by him, that she wanted to care for him in the same way that he cared for her, that she was not to be pitied but that she was just as capable of loving as he was.

Ivan stood up and looked into Jasmina's eyes again. " I know, I love you. I know that, and it's impossible for me to explain this to you but my faith will not allow me to marry you…"

She tried to protest but he looked at her pleadingly and continued.

" …But I know this. I will never love again. I cannot love again after this and every part of my heart and soul and body agonizes to be yours and for you to be mine. I love you. I love you. I love you."

He broke down and suddenly found himself being held gently in the warmth of Jasmina's arms. She whispered in his ear, "I love you too, and I will seek to know more about God in the way you do. You are clean. I want to have that cleanness. I know that no one will marry me because I have been defiled. But I will love you in my heart, there will never be goodbyes with us because wherever I go you will always be in my heart."

    Gently at first and then in a deeper almost convulsive way they both began to weep. Great sobs of injustice and pain tempered with a desire to do what was right flowed over them as they stood together in the silence of the room. Ivan walked over to the table, opened the drawer and took out his Bible. He held it out to Jasmina without saying a word.

# 8
## Finding Peace

Marija held the telephone in her hand, barely able to believe what she was hearing. She said nothing to Ivan about her visit to the priest. " I know this is going to be very hard for you to process and I thought I should ask you first. I can be over in about an hour."

As she hung up the telephone she could feel herself shaking. She walked over to the mirror and looked at herself. She thought back to the night that she had told her husband that she was pregnant. He had been so excited. They had laughed together and to an onlooker they would have appeared immature, almost silly, in the way that they had teased each other. He would insist on her sitting down then take off her slippers and rub her feet. She would laugh, and though times were hard with the war just beginning, life had been so simple in terms of love and expectations. Now as she looked at herself in the mirror it was all different. Her husband was dead, her baby gone. She was alone and craved love yet could not pursue it. She longed for intimacy yet knew that it could be found only in love not in some casual relationship. Yet to love seemed to be an impossibility.  The priest's words about finding a vulnerable Serb had been haunting her and now one was being delivered to her doorstep! There was a knock at the door and she immediately looked at the clock, amazed that an hour had passed so quickly. As the door opened slowly she saw the form of Ivan standing there and just behind him, cowering beneath the emotional weight of the constant moving and changing that had been his life for the past several weeks, she saw a little boy. His large eyes were dark gray, his hair was untidy with fugitive strands hanging down in front of his face.

Ivan smiled, kissing his sister on both cheeks. " Marija, this is Stefan. Stefan this is Marija." Stefan held out his hand and as his young fingers met Marija's own she felt tenderness equal in strength to the hatred that she had felt that other night at the church when she had spat and cursed and thrown stones.

As Stefan walked in she found herself placing her hand on his shoulder. " Well, let's start this right by making something to eat."

Stefan looked searchingly into Marija's face. It was if he were looking to see if there was pity or contempt, love or disgust. He nodded, placed his hand on his heart then very gently smiled.

# 9

## The Doorway

Marija handed Ivan the phone. He could see from the corner of his eye that Stefan was curled up asleep in the bedroom. Marija motioned to him to speak softly so as not to wake him. Ivan waved her away. He had said to her the previous week that she was treating the boy like a baby and that he was a growing lad and not to be pampered. She ignored him completely and had already, in her heart, crossed a barrier when she realized that she loved Stefan like a son. The paperwork had come through so she could adopt him, even though he was a Serb.

Ivan shrugged his shoulders and spoke into the phone. " Darko, tell me everything." Darko's voice was as usual satirical in style. " Well, Zagreb, you are the man as they say in Toyland. Everyone has been talking about it but I put them straight. I said to them, 'Zagreb is like salt and light, he shines and purifies and melts the snow.' But the big news is that I think your woman is interested in one of her own kind. Hope it's OK to say it outright like that."

Ivan felt as if he was going to throw up. He knew that Darko had little or no capacity for sensitivity but this was a terrible piece of news, delivered so brutally that the pain seemed to hit him in the face. The voice at the end of the phone continued relentlessly, "We just had someone down to show some videos including the new one from Toyland, 'Beauty and the Beast." Well, I think that's what's going on here. You remember that Muslim guy who came in almost headless? What a mess! Anyway, apparently he was the kid who saved her in the jungle when the Arkan Brigade was leaving its mark

## Jasmina, Darko and Milena

on the table of history. Well, it seems Burek is thicker than water and they are, as they say in Mickey and Minnie's home town, a couple."

The rest of the conversation detailing other events in the camp was a blur to Ivan. He hung up the phone, made his excuses to his sister and walked out into the gray night. There was a drizzle hanging in the air. He walked as fast as he could, initially to try to burn off the pain building up inside. He tried to pray but found it impossible. His mind was filled with a kaleidoscope of thoughts and images. He knew he could never marry Jasmina, yet he loved her. If he loved her then he should wish the best for her, and to love someone like this boy who was all smashed up was good. Because he was in such a bad way then he would be open to marrying her. Maybe he, Ivan, could become a friend to them both, wish them well and seek to share his faith with them. No that was crazy. He loved her and in the drama of the moment he had committed himself never to love again. He was committed to her and only to her. He could not forget her or forget the sense of electricity that had flowed right through him when she had held him in her arms on the last day. He could still hear her voice, telling him she loved him and that wherever he was he would always be in her heart.

He started to cry and tried to walk faster and faster. He was abruptly interrupted as someone addressed him. " Excuse me are you all right? You look very troubled."

A short elderly man with a long black raincoat was standing on the corner of the street. The road wet with mist and drizzle reflected a streetlight that gave an almost otherworldly context to the stranger's words. The old man continued to speak. "Let's sit down over here and talk." The persuasiveness of his manner and the authority that came with his age acted like a magnet to Ivan's broken heart. There was a bench under a tree and the two sat down quietly. The old man introduced himself, holding out his hand. " Mr. Gabriel, but my friends call me Gabby."

Ivan sat silent, this old man seemed more like someone to be addressed as sir rather than Gabby.

Mr. Gabriel gave Ivan a penetrating look before speaking very softly. " A broken heart, if I am not mistaken ? " Ivan looked back at him. Who was he, an angel? Yet he found himself slowly warming to the old man and over the next several minutes told his story.

At times he found himself unable to control the tears, at other times he just felt a sense of great relief at being able to unburden himself. The old man sat nodding in empathy and compassion.

As Ivan came to the end of his story the old man put his hand on his shoulder. The mist and drizzle had cleared and the stars were visible in the night sky. " Well, this is quite a story. Let me ask you some questions. If you love this girl so much why don't you just ask her to marry you, leave your job and take her as your wife?"

Ivan looked at the ground. He had asked himself that same question over and over again in his mind. He loved God, he wanted to serve the Jesus who meant so much to him, but he also longed for this young woman so deeply. "I'm a Christian, and by that I mean not just someone who goes to church because it's my culture, but because I have had my life affected dramatically by Jesus. It's hard to explain, but I know I cannot marry someone who does not believe what I believe in the same way."

The old man nodded. " Isn't that a little narrow minded?" Ivan smiled ruefully. " It is narrow minded, perhaps, but it's also very practical. Imagine the conflict of two people who love each other deeply yet are unable to be united in the deepest and most fundamental part of life, their belief in God."

The old man leaned back and looked up at the stars. " Well, if you love her so much but can't marry her, then you have only three options." He paused for what seemed a very long time. Ivan wanted answers, not silence. He urged the old man on by his body language. " The three options are simple, you can give up your belief in God as you understand it now, you can marry her with your beliefs, or you can show love to her by being her friend and wishing her the best with this new man she is friends with whose faith is the same as hers."

Ivan was about to respond when the old man stood up, taking his hand from Ivan's shoulder as he did so. " Don't say anything, just do what is right."

He turned and walked slowly down a side street and, as suddenly as he had come into Ivan's life, he was gone. The young man stood in the street unaware of the hum of the city around him. He looked into the sky and for just a moment he felt alone. Then a sense of destiny enveloped his soul. He turned and walked back towards his sister's home. He needed to be near Stefan, for the boy was his one link with Jasmina. He needed to be near his sister and feel her love. He prayed slowly and silently as he walked. Three options in the form of questions kept filling his mind.

# 10
## Ivan's Bible

Nadji Mehmedovic sat on a chair in the small room where Jasmina was staying. The other residents were out so they were alone. Jasmina sat cross-legged on the floor. She was now wearing Bosnian clothing, which was so much more comfortable. She had begun to gain weight and looked healthier. Her eyes, though, were filled with sadness. Nadji, whose face was badly disfigured, looked across at her and smiled.

"Don't misunderstand me when I say this, but you are a village girl, yet not a village girl. The words you use, the way you speak, well, you know."

Jasmina smiled playfully. " Well it's a long story. My father...." She paused, feeling again the pain of her father's absence. "My father was from a Gypsy area in Sarajevo and under the communists he decided to get out of the city and move to the villages to have a more simple life. He married my mother who really was a simple yet lovely woman, but he was the one who really raised and educated us children. So we were strangers in the village in some ways. Even though we did not have money we were, as you say, different in the way we speak."

She looked out of the window. It was beginning to snow. " That is why it has been so hard to have this Christian friend who maybe... well no Muslim would marry me, and I could never have married into village life anyway, well not easily."

## Jasmina, Darko and Milena

Nadji nodded understandingly. "But why is it such a problem for him to marry someone who does not believe like he does? Seems very narrow minded to me. My wife believes differently from me. She is a good Muslim and I am a bad Muslim it's as simple as that!"

Jasmina smiled again. She liked Nadji. He loved his little boy and his wife, who by a strange coincidence was also called Jasmina but was in constant terror, not knowing if they were alive or dead. He was safe, though, for her. No one bothered them that they were together. She was grateful to him as he had saved both her own and Stefan's life. He had laughed loudly when he heard the story of Stefan being a Serb pretending to be a Muslim.

There was a knock on the door and Darko walked in. Seeing the two of them alone together he nodded without smiling and excused himself. As he walked away he thought again what a shame it was for Ivan, but it was better this way. Burek is thicker than water, he thought to himself.

Ivan knelt by his bed and prayed. " Oh Lord, three options, just three options. I want to do what is right but I long for this girl with my heart and with my body and soul. Give me the strength to do what is right. I love her but I have to let go. She can find happiness with this man and perhaps I can share with them something of your love and mercy."

The other people in the unit were sleeping. A single bulb next to Jasmina's bunk gave enough light to read by. She sat holding Ivan's Bible. She had no idea where to begin. So she started at the first page, which made no sense at all. It seemed to be talking about some religious society. She flicked through the pages reading bits and pieces here and there but nothing caught her attention.

## The Roma Chronicles

She closed the Bible and lay on her bed looking at the late snow that was softly and gently bathing the outside world with its pure whiteness. She thought of God and of her feelings. She could identify that she felt dirty and unclean in herself, but knew that it was not her fault, yet somehow she felt as if she had guilt beyond that single horrific event. It made no sense. She hated the man who had done this to her yet she still felt some kind of guilt. Mercifully sleep came upon her as she put the Bible on a shelf next to her bed.

Ivan lay on his bed looking at the ceiling. In his mind he went over the times when he had been with Jasmina. He cried and agonized mentally, praying as he fell asleep, " Lord, help Jasmina to find you, not because I want her, she's probably already connecting with this other man, but Lord I pray for her that she would know what it is to know you and to know what it is to be at peace with God."

Marija sat at her desk and wrote in her diary. Her broken heart had begun to heal since Stefan had come to live with her. In him she had someone on whom to pour out all the love that resided inside her. She ached, however for Ivan who was so sad. He seemed to be in love with this Gypsy girl but his faith was so deep that he could not allow himself to pursue the idea of being married to her. She put her pen down and looked upwards with closed eyes. " Oh God, wherever you are, help us all."

Jasmina suddenly sat upright in bed, almost hitting her head on the bunk above her. She was sweating. This dream was so different from the others, the ones that had tormented her. As she lay on the bed sweating her mind relived the dream that seemed still so graphic.

In this dream she had been back in her village and saw the little white dove that had been so close to her. She remembered how she had wanted the fragile creature to fly away before it was hurt. In the dream she was not beaten or abused but dressed in a flowing long white gown that seemed to sparkle with purity. The air was filled with freshness and a sense of peace and joy. She had a great feeling of being washed and cleansed. The small dove was with her and seemed to know what was going on. There were other birds too and spring was all around her.

Suddenly, she turned and saw herself in the same place but now it was winter and everything was gloomy, cold and wet. She was wearing dark, shabby, torn clothes that stank. She could remember that in the dream they smelt horrible of death and darkness. Then in an instant the white dove seemed to be speaking with her, although not with words, communicating something that she could understand intuitively. 'Come over and leave the darkness of spiritual winter behind. The darkness is not what has been done to you. The darkness is your inability to love God. Come away and know the spring of God's love and forgiveness'. Then she woke up. She looked over at the Bible on the shelf, picked it up once more and tried letting it open anywhere and started reading but still nothing seemed to make sense. She lay back down on the bed slowly, closing her eyes and praying again. " Oh God, speak to me, tell me what it means."

# 11

## The White Dove

Ivan walked towards the main train station. The day was cold, the air icy and an overcast sky suggested that anything could happen with the weather. He was hoping that Darko would give him some updates on Jasmina and also take her a letter that he had written the night before.

He was slowly coming to terms with the fact that he was never going to be able to love Jasmina in the fullest possible way. He found himself longing for her to have the sense of freedom that could come only from knowing God at that deeper level. He had struggled mentally and prayed about how best he could put into words what he wanted to say. He saw Darko walking across the road towards him. " Zagreb, why do you people love this place so much? Diesel fumes, gray skies, Blue Hats down dark alleyways, what an awful place! And I chose my one measly day off to spend time in this jungle, and I'm starving!"

Ivan laughed and hugged his friend. They made their way first to a Pizza place and then westwards by tram to where Marija lived. They looked from the tram at a city in the throes of redefining itself. Darko looked at the new statue of the Count on his horse with outstretched sword in defiance.

"I tell you, popular fiction will have to change, young lovers will no longer be saying, 'Meet me under the clock at midnight, now they'll be saying' Meet me under the horse. It doesn't sound right! I hope we don't lose that clock."

Ivan smiled as he looked at his friend. In some strange way

being with him brought him closer to Jasmina in his heart. He smiled as he spoke. " I have to say I miss our camp, Darko, where I am now is almost sterile in comparison. Most of my time up here is spent working on papers. I miss the people."

The tram made its way through the streets and finally deposited pilgrim and poet just a few meters from Marija's apartment block. The door opened and Marija stood smiling in the entrance. In the background Stefan was sitting reading a comic book. Immediately Marija's eyes caught Darko off guard and he found himself stuttering and star struck as he was introduced.

They sat down but Darko's discomfort was very apparent. He thought to himself that he had never in his life seen a woman so beautiful and so full of character. Stefan joined the group and there was much talk about how he was doing and the great news that the authorities were going to allow Marija to adopt him with few problems.

They laughed as they said how different it would be after all the wars were over and the south Slavs rediscovered the bureaucracy which would make them feel safe again.

Darko walked over to the bookshelf and scanned the titles. He took out a book that was obviously profound and commented on it to Marija. Ivan looked on amazed. Darko, the carefree guy who could never be serious, was right now talking to his sister about some fine point of philosophy. She nodded as he spoke and seemed as smitten with him as he was with her. Ivan prayed silently, " Lord, this is a strange world."


Jasmina walked alone through the camp, her mind filled with wonder. She struggled with the deep issues in her heart. What did that dream really mean? Was this God speaking to her or was it just her subconscious, dragging up these images from within? It was good to be alone and quiet for a while.

She enjoyed talking with Nadji but he was so longing for his wife and trying to recover from his wounds that it was difficult to be around him. She craved silence for it was only in the silence that she could really think deeply. It was here that she could wrestle with these things that were plaguing her. She thought back to the terrible night when she was defiled and her family destroyed. For the first time she realized that she was using the dreadful things that had happened to her as an excuse to cover up things about herself she did not like.

She remembered her reaction when her sister came in saying she would one day marry a young man in the village, how Jasmina did not want such a marriage for herself. It was OK for her sister, maybe, but Jasmina felt that she was of a higher class, and needed to go to a larger city and marry someone more intelligent.

She thought about her mother's occasional chats with their neighbors and how Jasmina had felt their conversation was so empty and how she had not wanted to be like them because she felt superior to them. Her mind began to dredge up from deep within herself a whole series of attitudes that made her feel very ashamed of herself.

As these issues came up one by one she realized that as a victim she had an excuse. No one could think badly of her because she had experienced such a terrible ordeal. Perhaps, just perhaps, the significance of the dream was that God was showing her that the dirty smelly clothes were not the defilement of what had happened to her at the hands of evil men, but rather the real her, which was not the lovely girl that everyone thought her to be.

She touched the scar on her forehead, carved as a sign of contempt. For a moment she stood still looking away towards the fields on the edge of the camp. Perhaps, she reflected, that scar should be on the inside of her heart to signify the contempt she now felt for herself for being so selfish and superior. If only people knew what she was really like inside they would not pity her.

Nothing was said on the tram after leaving Marija's apartment. Darko was pensive, Ivan confused. As they arrived at the train station it was Ivan who broke the silence. "I've never seen you like this before. You were utterly zapped by my sister. Poetry, philosophy and …" He changed his voice, imitating his friend's intellectual tone: "I agree with you Marija, Nadia Jonke is the best kept secret in the national Opera House. Opera House! All you ever talk to me about is blue pee!"

Darko sighed, "Your sister is the most beautiful person I have ever met, but she needs to be away from a guy like me, she has a long way to go before she can love again."
He suddenly reverted to his usual flippant mode. "And one of you must surely be adopted as there's no way that the same womb could produce…"

Ivan punched his friend in the arm and then became serious. He reached into his coat pocket and took out an envelope.
" Can you give this to Jasmina for me?" Darko nodded. " Sure, but you know that she and…." " I know, I know, but just give her this for me, please."

The two friends embraced and Darko ran to catch his train. Ivan walked up to the city's main square. He wondered if he would meet Mr. Gabriel again and if he would be able to talk with him. As he walked he thought about how complex life was.

He sensed that his feelings towards Jasmina were undergoing a change. Instead of longing for her as his wife, he was now longing for her to know peace with God. He knew that the hardest thing ever for someone as gentle and sweet as Jasmina would be to see that she needed God in terms of forgiveness. The whole idea of

Jesus dying as a punishment for sin, her sin, would be so hard to grasp. These things all seemed like symbols. The idea that man was separated from God because of sin was the hardest of all barriers for anyone to cross. To see themselves no matter how good they were by human standards, as rotten in the sight of God was something that only the Spirit of God Himself could reveal.

    He found himself praying for her, praying that, if she and this other man were to come together, they could find the peace that only comes from having one's sins forgiven by God.

# 12
## Confusion

Nadji came bursting into Jasmina's unit, shouting at the top of his voice, "They found my wife and son! They found my wife and son! They're bringing them here!"

At this he slumped onto his knees and started crying. He thought of his dead friends who would never be reunited with their loved ones. Jasmina, also in tears, came over to comfort and rejoice with him. He looked up through his tears, his face distorted and broken. Jasmina knew what he was thinking.

"She will think that you have never looked so handsome in all your life." Nadji knelt upright, still sobbing.

The whole camp turned out to see the emotional reunion. TV cameras were there and the entire camp seemed to set aside the frustrations of life for a brief season of joy as many lived vicariously through what Nadji and his wife were experiencing. They wept in each other's arms. She touched his broken face, kissed his wounds and cried some more. Their little boy was held between them, clasping the daddy he thought was gone forever.

When things had settled down a little, the TV presenter spoke. " And so Nadji and Jasmina Ahmedovic are man and wife in a refugee camp far from home yet filled with hope for the future."

Jasmina slowly opened the letter from Ivan. She smiled and wept as she read his warm and kind introduction. Then suddenly she gasped. The letter read, "….. I have been praying for you and for your study of the Bible I gave you. Then something came to mind. In the Bible there is a beautiful story of two people who love each other, which is an allegory of the way God loves us as people. It's called 'The Song of Solomon', I checked and I have the same edition of the Bible as you and on page 654 you will find that it says this: ' Come away my love, my fair one, for the winter is past, the rain is gone and the sound of the dove is singing in the land….' "

Jasmina could not believe her eyes. It was just like her dream! She read and reread it again and again. How could he have known? He couldn't have done… so it must be, somehow it must be God speaking to her! She continued to read and wept again as he told her that he must now be separated from her and that if she chose to marry someone else in the camp, then he longed for them both to know Jesus.

She was confused by this, not understanding what he was referring to, but kept returning to the part of the letter in which he had written about the dove. She ran to her bunk, took the Bible from the little shelf and turned to the page. There it was, as plain as could be.

" Ivi, hi it's me." Ivan smiled as his sister used her childhood name for him. " Hey listen, I thought I should call you immediately because I was just watching the news and they had your camp on. I didn't get the whole story but they had a couple on there and they were saying something about being far from home but Mr. Nadji and Mrs. Jasmina Ahmedovic were looking for a hope for tomorrow or something. The guy had his face all smashed up from a war wound. Sorry Ivan darling, but is this?"

" Yes, that is them." Ivan fought to keep his composure. He wanted to give the pain to God, but his voice broke. " Oh Marija, it hurts so bad. I love her so much."

## Jasmina, Darko and Milena

Only the sound of his quiet weeping could be heard on the telephone as Marija assured him of her love and told him that she understood.

The plaintive melody of Stefan's pipe could be heard in the background. Ivan hung up the phone, walked across the room and then fell or rather collapsed onto the floor before crawling into a kneeling position by the side of his bed.

He began to pound his fists on the bed. " It's not fair! It's not fair! God, it's not fair! Why did you let me fall in love with her knowing that we could never be together?" He hit the bed with his fist again. "If you were my son, I wouldn't let this happen to you."

The dam broke and a great primal cry of soul pain emerged from the deepest reaches of his person. He kept repeating Jasmina's name.

Jasmina sat with the Bible in front of her, reading the verses over and over again. She flipped through the pages knowing that somewhere in this book lay answers. She had encountered the supernatural in a profound and personal way. She now knew that God was alive and real. She knew that he was involved in her life because of the dream and the letter from Ivan; it was too much to be a coincidence. She realized that God was using Ivan and his Bible and that this Christian God, this Jesus, was somehow real in the middle of the complexity. She realized too that there was a definite connection with the awareness that had come to her recently of seeing herself not as someone good but rather as someone who was not like God. Now the question seemed to be, "What do I do now? Where do I go with this information for a more full and complete understanding?"

She looked out of the window, hearing the continuing music

and celebration for Nadji and his wife. She opened her Bible again, but it was so large, so much of it just names and places that she did not understand. Then it occurred to her that Darko was a Christian, he had to be because he was a Croat. He would know where to turn to in this Holy Book. She quickly put a coat on and ran down to his office.

" Well, technically I'm a Christian in that I was baptized, but I'm not like Ivan, who is really 'into' his religion." Darko was surprised that he was being asked to instruct a Muslim girl on how to find the truth of Christianity. "But I guess if you want to know what Christianity is all about…" He thought for a moment, " I suppose you should read about Jesus in the Gospels."

Her expression made him realize that she was a blank slate. " OK in the second part of the book there is a section called the New Testament and at the beginning of that there are four smaller sections called Matthew, Mark, Luke and John. Those are the gospels they tell the stories about Jesus."
He reached for a pen and wrote the names down. "Happy pilgrimage."

Back in the unit Jasmina turned the pages of the book until she discovered one of the names, Luke, there it was just as Darko had said. She wrote down the page number. The sense of excitement was almost overpowering as she began to read about Jesus.

She read for hours, going back over certain passages several times so that she got the idea. The stories enchanted her, the love and kindness of Jesus, his interest in women as people not as objects. His love for children and the incredible parables took her breath away.

She collapsed back onto her bed and closed her eyes.
" This teacher is the greatest of all! I will follow him, now I know why Ivan is like he is."

# 13

## Redemption

After taking the two-hour train journey into Zagreb again on his day off, Darko slowly walked up the steps to Ivan's room, and knocked on the door. Inside Ivan looked at the clock, wondering who on earth would be knocking at this time of the morning. Since settling into his new job in the camp on the outskirts of Zagreb his small room had become a place to retreat and be quiet, to think, to pray and to read. He called out for the person to identify himself. A muffled voice responded that it was the health inspector.

Ivan opened the door to see Darko standing there. Ivan spoke first. " Don't tell me…. You want to see what color…"
" Zagreb, I bring you news that should take your pathetic, miserable, early morning and turn it into a blaze of sunshine." Ivan smiled through his tiredness. "Come in and I'll make coffee."

" Well, Zagreb, I have misinformed you, I'm afraid. Firstly Nadji Hole-in-the-Headovich was in fact already married and only a platonic associate of your friend Jasmina, and secondly…."

Ivan raised his voice, " Don't mess with my feelings, man this is not good what you're doing." Darko raised his hands in defense. " The truth, the truth my old, urban, gray skinned friend." Ivan looked intensely into Darkos face. " But my sister called me! She saw them on television, they were married at the camp." Darko laughed and then replied. " Ah, my friend, your sister is more noble than you will ever be but what she probably saw was the interview with Hole-in-the-Headovich whose wife is also called Jasmina… and because your sister, endowed with more intellect than you will ever aspire

68

to, never saw the real Jasmina, she must have assumed that the new Jasmina was in fact the old Jasmina…"

Ivan turned to Darko laughing and crying simultaneously, then rushed into the other room as Darko called after him. "Also, your Jasmina is a student of your religion. She had the good sense to come to me for spiritual counsel but alas, all I could do was point her in the direction of the Good Book."

Ivan lay prostrate on floor in prayer. He cried out to God to save Jasmina for His sake but also for his, Ivan's, sake. "Oh Jesus, you are working. I can feel it. Bring Jasmina to yourself and please, oh Lord, please let me be her husband."

There was a knock on the door and he heard Darko's voice again. " Did I do right or wrong?"

Ivan continued to lie motionless on the floor, but whispered. " You did right, you did right."


Darko sat in Marija's apartment talking about art and music. Stefan was sitting in the corner with his pipe, playing a tune. "With all this talk about religion these days, what are you going to do for the boy? He's Orthodox. Will you bring him up Orthodox?"

Marija smiled. " I've thought a lot about it and I was wondering if we could talk about it? Maybe you can give me some advice."

Darko smiled in response, "I think that actually your brother has something that is deeper than any of these religious traditions Muslim, Protestant, Catholic, Orthodox. It's so real to him. You know, he's perfectly normal yet he lives and breathes his faith. Maybe let Stefan have his Orthodox cultural traditions but also what shall we call it? Ivan spirituality." Marija looked seriously. " It's strange you should say that," Marija replied, "because these last few months have made me think about life and death and how we should live, but I'd never thought of it quite like that. Keep your traditions, whatever they are, but have Ivan spirituality. Do you know I don't even know what kind of a church he goes to."

Ivan entered at this point and passed a thick envelope to his friend. " Lose it and I will kill you slowly with blunt instruments." Darko raised his eyebrows and looked at Marija.
" Maybe the Peace For All Christian Fellowship?"


Nadji sat alone in the room with his wife, a simple village girl. She quietly reached out her hand and touched his face. "You are the most handsome man in the world."

He looked at the floor and then gazed into her eyes. The long night of suffering was not over for them but it had passed into a new stage where at least some light could be seen in the future. He thought of his friends who were now gone. He wondered where they were now in some after life. An unsettling sense of sadness filled him despite the almost overwhelming euphoria of the reunion with his wife and son.


Jasmina tore open the letter from Ivan and read the words with both joy and contemplation. She opened her Bible and followed the page numbers that he had given. She had read of the life of Jesus and she loved him as her teacher and master. She had read about how he was taken away and crucified, nailed to a wooden cross. She wept in anger and frustration as she read that story.

Then, when it came to the place where Jesus came up from death and was alive again, she started to laugh with joy. Someone looked through the window and saw her and hurried on. She did not care for she was finding God and as she was looking for God she was discovering Jesus. This coming back to life after his death had so moved her. The first person he appeared to was Mary a woman not unlike her ruined by life itself.

She followed Ivan's explanations and instructions in the letter very carefully. The letter was all about sin and being set free from sin and being reconciled to God. She had been correct, those bad feelings she was having about herself were right. She was unclean not because of what had happened to her but because of something in herself that seemed to be all wrong.

She read on. Jesus dying on the cross was God's way of punishing our sin so that our spirits, our consciences and our whole lives could be forgiven and made right before God.

Ivan shared the story of how a little Gypsy girl had come to the camp and he had befriended her. She, like Stefan, had been given a pipe to learn to play. He shared how one day she had run into his office so excited because she had learned to play a tune that she wanted to play for him. After she had given her performance she had gone up to him and hugged him and rubbed her hair against his face as they embraced. She had run out of the office with joy.

Ivan then confessed that she had been so dirty that he had found himself instinctively going over to the sink to wash his hands and face. Suddenly it came to him that this is what God is like. We are all dirty. Even with our greatest acts of love and worship we are unclean before a pure and Holy God. Our greatest acts of goodness are still not enough to bring us clean before a Holy God. It has to be God reaching down to us forgiving our sins because he loves us. It was the same for Jasmina. It was not something she could ever do for herself, that would make her self acceptable to God but it had already been done for her.

It had been done for her! She paused and cried out. "I

understand." A deep peace that she was forgiven began to flow over her soul. God was so real she could sense his presence in the room.

"Forgive me, cleanse me, have mercy on me, a sinner. You are my God, you are my Lord, you are my Savior."

She lay down quietly and closed her eyes. She could feel the dove, she could feel the white clothes, all pure, childlike and clean and fresh.

# 14

## The Question

Jasmina sat in Marija's apartment. Everyone, had left so that the couple could be alone to talk. Marija, Stefan and Darko went out for dinner and to be together. Darko and Marija had become at this point the closest of friends. Stefan was happy, truly happy for the first time in his short life. Ivan sat quietly and listened to the whole story. His eyes would well up with tears and then he would compose himself as she continued. She told him of her dream, his letter, the burden of her sin and the sense of God providing in Jesus the release from that sin. She thanked him for his kindness and his gentleness. She thanked him again for being different from the other men in the camp and for the way he had looked at her that made her feel pure rather than the way that others looked at her.

She looked to the window and smiled, almost wondering as if a dove would fly by. " I shall never be able to ever tell you how much my heart has been relieved. I still can't seem to connect with the fact that my parents, brother and sister are not alive. I worry about their souls and how it is too late for them to hear yet in my heart I know that God does what is right, and that gives me comfort."

Ivan walked over to where she was sitting and knelt before her. "I love you Jasmina. I love you with a love that wants to serve you, care for you, protect you and be your companion in life." He paused and looked into her eyes. "I offer you my love, and I want to marry you Jasmina. I want to be your husband. I know you still have a long way to go putting all the past behind you but I want to walk there with you. But if you should need more time, then I …."

Jasmina reached out her hand and placed it on his lips.

" I want to be your wife. I love you. You have shown me the face of God."

Ivan looked into her eyes again. He felt as if he could see into her soul, this precious one who had suffered so much. He reached up to her forehead and kissed her scar. " I love you unutterably."

His voice quivered as he spoke. He drew her to himself and held her in his arms as he continued to kneel before her. He could hear her heartbeat, and prayed in time to its beat, "Oh Lord, thank you, thank you, thank you."

# 15

## The Kiss

Jasmina stood next to Nadji, who was giving her away in marriage, taking her father's place. His wife, the other Jasmina, her bridesmaid, stood beside her. Slowly walking towards her was Ivan with Darko as his best man. Her eyes met his and they stayed locked together as if embracing each other in a way that went beyond the mere physical.

Ivan experienced a degree of love and affection for her that he would not have believed possible. He wanted to cry out that he loved her and that even though he was only human he would choose every day to serve her, love her and do all within his power to make her life one of peace and joy.

She looked at him with respect and honor realizing that she loved this man with a love deeper than anything she had ever read or heard about. He had only to look at her for her to feel it.

The next moments seemed to be over in a flash as they pledged their love to each other and were pronounced man and wife. Ivan cupped Jasmina's face in his hands and slowly drew her face towards his. Her mouth quivered and parted slightly as he placed his lips on hers for the first time. He gently drew back, and then kissed the scar on her forehead. Barely a person was not weeping openly. The flow of love between them seemed to encompass the whole church. In a daze they walked out into the street. Marija stood in front of them just a few meters away. The sun was shining and there was a freshness and joy about the day that made it one to remember for a lifetime.

## The Roma Chronicles

Marija raised her hand for quiet as the guests arranged themselves around the couple in a half circle on the steps of the church. In the quietness the sound of a melody could be heard. Seated cross-legged on a bench was Stefan playing the pipe that Ivan had given him. Tears slowly trickled down his face as he poured all the feeling that was in him into the tune.

The melody came to an end and Marija lifted a box and opened the flap. Three white doves gently ascended towards the sky.

## Part Two
## Darko
## To Love and To Be Loved

# 1

## The Visitor

Darko's new flat was simple yet comfortable. There was, as often is the case with the emotionally complex, a sense of confusion between how it was decorated and his actual personality.

He was constantly accused of not taking life seriously and often appeared to be observing life rather than participating in it. Despite this, his flat was decorated with the most sophisticated and sensitive prints of modern artists and the design and the color scheme would be more at home in Milan than in New Zagreb. There were several originals by lesser-known artists in the style of Naïve Art with winter scenes of hard working peasants with large feet and hands painted on glass. In the center of one of the walls was Darko's prize piece. It was a simple line drawing of a flower. In the bottom right corner it was signed and dedicated, To Darko from Ivan Lackovich Croata. Darko had grown up close to Djurdjevac where the artist was from and had met him at an exhibition as a child. For Darko to be surrounded by his art and his friends was his ultimate joy.

This evening if anyone had walked in on the home and saw the group assembled, they would have been forgiven for thinking this was a body of people who were innocent of the horrors of war. The opposite was true as each of them had seen or experienced suffering at the deepest levels.

Despite this there was an air of human celebration of the kind that comes when several people of deep character draw together. It is as if everyone's strengths are poured into a single atmosphere that all present bathe within. The warmth of the room, the smell of coffee and fresh fruit and the soft music playing as a back drop made this either a picture of heaven or its alternative.

Ivan and Jasmina had been married for six months. They acted as if it was just six hours but at the same time they were relaxed with each other as if they had been friends for a lifetime. Jasmina held Ivan's hand and continually stroked it. Every so often without being conscious of it she would lift his hand to her face and kiss it. He in turn would pause periodically and just look into her eyes with devotion and caring.

Marija sat next to Darko. They were in love at the deepest possible level but Darko wanted to move very slowly in their relationship, as the death of her husband in the war and loss of their unborn child were still areas of pain close to the surface of her heart.

She was happy. She was happy that her brother had married Jasmina. Jasmina was so gentle and good that it made the motherly feelings towards her brother expand into an overall warmth and peace. She was happy that now the adoption of Stefan had gone through and that the void in her life for a child had been filled.

Stefan had adjusted so well and was so at peace despite not being able to speak and anyone would have thought that she was his natural mother. She was in love with Darko. He was so patient despite his constantly joking. He gave her the sense of safety that only love and care could produce.

Darko gently tapped on his glass with a spoon and then stood up. He raised his glass and then with a dramatic clearing of his throat began his speech. "Ladies and Gentlemen I propose a toast to the most celebrated couple in this smoky run-down city which we call the capital of our new and bright ..." Ivan made a snoring noise that caused the girls to burst into laughter. "You may mock and make light," Darko continued. "But this is a new day where dreams can become…" Marija laughingly interrupted, "We are hungry please finish." He had a look of stunned impatience and continued. "Is it not a new day that has come, Ante Pavelic, Josip the Broz and Tanja Torbarina are all covered by this new Republic where blood and Burek flow with freedom and…"

The doorbell interrupted him. He spoke as he walked looking at Ivan. "Zagreb you have been saved from certain obesity by the bell."

He opened the door and standing in front of him was a young Roma boy about fourteen years old. The shock of seeing the young boy caused Darko to step back as if he had suddenly been slapped in the face. An almost icy atmosphere of confusion immediately descended upon the group. The young boy spoke but in a language the others could not understand. Darko instinctively replied in the same language and then motioned for the young boy to come into the flat. He then pointed to a side room and spoke to the young man once more in the unknown language.

The others watched and were silent. It was as if a knife had suddenly cut into the safety of the atmosphere and taken them all back to a world of war and death that they knew so well. No one spoke the whole time Darko was in the room with the young man. They could hear the mumble of their conversation aware that even if it were spoken in front of them they would be locked out from understanding.

Once more the door opened and Darko walked across to the front door and let the young man out. Just as he was leaving he reached into his pocket and gave the young man a 50 Kuna note. As the door closed he leaned back against it with his eyes closed.

His friends watched him as he tried to gather himself together walking the few meters across the room to where they were sitting. He sat down as everyone's eyes were fixed upon his pale shaken face.

Ivan was the first to speak. "Do want to talk about this or would you prefer that we go?"

Darko closed his eyes and squeezed them shut trying to create a barrier for the tears that had formed and now had spilled over onto his cheeks. Marija reached out her hand and held his firmly but gently, she spoke almost in a whisper. "What is it? What is wrong?"

He leaned towards her and laid his head on her shoulder. She in turn reached out and caressed his tired head as a mother would a sick child. He began to weep uncontrollably.

Slavitsa stood alone on the side of the road. She was wearing jeans and a yellow T-shirt and carried a small handbag that hung from her shoulder. The main road from Nagykanizsa to Zalakomar was an active place for prostitutes but the new road they were planning would mean she and the other girls would have to create new territory for themselves. Her main customers were truck drivers and they would disappear from these small roads once the highway was finished.

Her cell phone rang. Not many people had mobile phones. They were all the rage with business people but most thought it was a fad that would soon pass away. For her, the cell phone was business, the voice on the other end was Angela. She worked a small patch close by and was just keeping in touch.

Slavitsa liked Angela. She was not a Roma like herself but they were similar and every time they met they talked about getting out of the business and working together to open up a little flower shop. Once again she was standing alone as the cars and trucks rushed by her. None of the regulars had come by today. She hated being a prostitute but was a willing participant in an occupation that could earn her more money in a day than in a month working in a factory, even if she could find a job.

Once the line of selling oneself had been crossed it was as if some inward spiritual transaction had been made. There really was no turning back. The cell phone rang again. Standing alone by the side of the road she listened in silence and then began to cry.

The woman's body was laid out on the bed. She was wearing a cotton dress and a sweater. Behind the head of the bed were several collections of flowers, all around the body were cheap plastic candleholders, the light from the candles was the only light in the one room house.

Periodically people would come into the room and stand for a while next to the body. Two older men sat on chairs by the bed and from time to time would reach out and rearrange an arm or a leg of the dead woman. Just a few feet away by the far wall was an open coffin. The funeral people had come earlier and left it with instructions not to leave the body on the bed too long or it may take a strange shape as it cooled down and then it would be hard to get in the coffin.

An elderly man leaned against the doorpost as a gatekeeper for those who would come and go. He had a bottle of beer in one hand that he would raise to his mouth. He spoke to a young woman who seemed intelligent and almost well dressed. "Have you told the relatives?"
She nodded. "We sent Allen down to Zagreb to tell the son but he may not come." He answered, "He's the one who changed his name, no?" She said, "Yes, he is a good boy and you can't blame him for getting out of all of this." He said, "I know, I know. How about

the bad girl? Did you find her?"
"Yes, I called her from the corner shop. Making calls over to Hungary costs an arm and a leg."

  Stefan lay on his bed in his room, he could hear Marija on the telephone in the other room. She seemed worried. He looked up at the ceiling. He loved the way that the shadows moved around because of the car lights in the street below reflecting on the windows.

    He held his wooden music pipe in his hand that Ivan had given to him. It had been for some time now his link between making sounds from the emotions that were locked inside of him.

    He found himself thinking of his upcoming visit to the hospital. They would do some tests to see if they could discover why he could not speak. He was afraid. He wanted to speak and be normal but he lived in a comfortable world where he knew how to survive. He was not sure if he wanted that to change. What he really wanted was his cross and chain back again that he had left in Bosnia. For some reason it connected his past life and his current world together. As he thought on these things he slowly drifted off to sleep.

# 2

## The Truth

Jasmina sat cross-legged on the floor leaning against an armchair. She held a mug of coffee in her hands. She was wearing, as she often did indoors, Bosnian village clothes. Her scarf was tied behind her head with her long auburn hair flowing down her back. Ivan was wearing running suit bottoms and a T-shirt. He also held a mug of coffee in his hands. He sat also on the floor leaning against the wall. They were both silent pondering what they had witnessed the night before.

Jasmina spoke first. "It is incredible, I just had no idea, no idea at all." Ivan smiled and then turned serious. "It does explain though why he was always joking. It is as if he was trying to lead us away from getting too close to him."

He paused sipped from the mug and then continued. "But you did not seem to understand the language at all why is that?"

Jasmina smiled and then replied. "I spoke what is called Arli growing up in the home and then Bosnian everywhere else. Darko's family is what we call the Rudari or they call themselves Bayash. Their language is like Romanian completely different than mine."

Ivan nodded. He looked at his wife and loved her so deeply. She was in his mind the most beautiful girl he had ever seen in his life. He then spoke. "So Darko Horvatich is really Darko Orshus. He changed his name and ran away from his culture and started a new life as a Croat. Incredible."

Jasmina put her coffee mug down and went to Ivan to lean upon him. He placed his arms around her and she felt safe. She kissed his hand and then spoke. "How does it make you feel, do you feel deceived?" He nodded and then replied. "No, not at all, I just feel the burden for him and also for Maria. I'm sure my parents will have something to say. A Roma daughter-in-law and perhaps a Roma son-in-law." He saw the funny side of it and laughed but then caught himself.

"I do feel for him with the news that his mother is dead and he has to go back to where he came from. It is going to be very hard for him."

Jasmina loved her husband he was such a good man she thought to herself. "Ivan, you know we love each other in this deep way."

He squeezed her in affection and kissed her on the top of the head. "Well, I do not take that love for granted you really are my master, you know I completely submit to you." He smiled. "You don't have to say that we are friends, lovers, companions and husband and wife." She closed her eyes with a sense of satisfaction upon her face and then spoke.

"I know, I know but I want you to know that. I want to ask your permission to do something."

He laughed without mockery. "You don't have to say it that way." She reached out and touched his hand. "I know but I would like to take Marija up to Darko's village and help them both. I know the Roma ways and I could help Marija especially learn about Roma things."

Ivan pondered for a moment. She was going to continue but he gently put his finger on her lips and then spoke. "Let me just think about this for a minute." They were both silent. He looked out of the window at the large tree that stood close to the flat they lived in. He loved these old trees that seemed so stable. He thought his children would grow up looking at this tree and it would always be there as a symbol of that which never changes.

He smiled and then looked at his wife. "OK, I have an idea. You go with Maria up to the Medjimurije and help her understand things and I will go down to Bosnia to your village and see if I can find your family's grave and Stefan's parent's grave and make sure that they are cared for."

Jasmina burst into tears and held onto to her husband tightly.

Marija drove through the heavy traffic on the way to the bus station. Darko sat next to her looking reflectively out of the window. "I'm sorry Maria I should have told you all of this earlier. I kept thinking I would wait for the right time but it never seemed to come."

She nodded, smiled and then spoke. "I've given you my heart Darko. I know you wanted to go slowly for my sake but it's too late for that. I've given you my heart."

He looked at her with sadness. "Do you feel betrayed by me?" "Not betrayed but confused. Why would you think that it would matter to me?"

He looked to his right as they came to the Dubrava tram stop. He could see through the window Roma women that were in a crouched position next to old clothes they were trying to sell.

"I've lived my whole life living a double life. It's so natural to me now that I'm not aware of the game I'm playing." Marija pursed her lips and then spoke. "It makes me afraid though that if you have kept this from me you may be keeping other things from me. I'm not Jasmina I don't naturally think good of everyone."

Darko was silent and in time they came to the bus station. "Just drop me off, parking is hopeless here I'll be okay."

Marija felt a sense of pain as he got out of the car. Almost immediately cars began to line-up behind them and started to sound their horns. Darko turned away and then back just as Marija was pulling away. He mouthed the word 'sorry' with his lips so she could see his sentiment without hearing him. He turned and quickly walked up the steps towards the ticket counters.


Slavitsa sat next to her mother's body. She rocked to and fro and made moaning noises periodically raising her voice and crying out to God asking Him why this had happened. Others from the village continued to come and go. They would stand for a while, some would go over to the body and lift a hand or stroke the face. More candles in cheap plastic holders were brought in and the whole room seemed to be filled with these and plastic bouquets of flowers.

Someone had brought a disposable camera and was taking pictures of the body and various ones standing next to it. The man who had earlier stood at the door with a bottle of beer was now propped up and sleeping on a chair in the corner of the room next to the empty coffin. He had a bag of cheese puffs in his hands opened but barely eaten. His snoring acted as comic backdrop to the scene of mourning. Occasionally children would come into the room and look at the body, some would carefully steal a cheese puff as they either entered or left.

The scene of normality in death was disturbed as a new black Mercedes pulled up outside the house. A large man with a blue suit, open shirt and gold chain hanging around his chest walked into the house and stood by the bed and next to Slavitsa. The man had a gold tooth in the front of his mouth that seemed to glitter as he spoke. "Sorry to see this – may she rest in peace."

Slavitsa did not move nor look up at the man. He spoke again. "You will have to carry on paying the installments for her. If you keep it going like you have been but add some more you can

## The Roma Chronicles

clear it in ten months."
Slavitsa continued to sit still and continued not responding.
 "If you try to get out of paying I will kill you and your brother."
          Slavitsa reached out and took her mother's lifeless hand and started to moan.  "We have people on the Hungarian side as well so there is no escape.  Anyway a young girl like you can make that money very easily."
 Slavitsa stood up and looked at the man.  She just nodded in agreement and then spoke.  "We need to put her in the coffin she's getting stiff."
The big man pointed to some of the other men standing by them and kicked the legs of the man sleeping holding the cheese puffs.  They gathered the dead woman up and roughly pushed her into the coffin.  It was a difficult fit and the men had to push and wedge her into place.


Marija sat next to Stefan in the hospital waiting room.  She tried to muster up as much courage and optimism as she could to cause him to relax.  He had never been in a hospital before and the hollow sounds of the voices and the footsteps created fear within him.  Marija's name was called and she and Stefan walked into a small examination room.  A nurse about Marija's age was in the corner preparing some surgical tools.  The sight of the various tools made Stefan afraid and he began to feel nauseous.
     A young doctor walked into the room and immediately caused him to feel at ease.  He was warm and friendly in his manner and Marija found herself saying a prayer of thanks despite her not feeling close to God these past 24 hours.  The kind doctor caused them both to relax and then very carefully the examination began.

# 3
## Coming Home

Darko undid his jacket as he stepped down from the air-conditioned bus into the early afternoon sunshine. The bus station had a tired and worn feeling to its atmosphere, which added to his immediate dislike of the town that he had spent so much of his childhood in.

He lit a cigarette and just stood still allowing himself to draw in warmth from the sun. The noise of the buses and smell of diesel fumes caused him not to linger but move on to his destination. He was going home. He decided to walk rather than catch another bus, as he wanted to try and clear his mind of all the conflicting emotions that were racing through it.

The sense of guilt he felt was like a heavy weight on his chest. He could not escape the feelings but he did not know how to process them. He looked at people as he walked. It felt as if everyone else around him was normal but he was a deceiver, someone who had concealed his identity for so long. He felt shame as well as frustration.

He thought of his mother. He had never really known her as he had been put into a foster home when he was just a small boy. He had gone back to the village at holidays but almost every time he visited she would be drunk. The man she was living with hated him and it was decided early on that he should not visit without a social worker to protect him.

It was his sister he loved and missed so much. He had not seen her now for nearly 8 years. He had written to her over the years and always left his address. For whatever reason he had not returned to the village and she had felt uncomfortable trying to visit him.

He was ashamed of his past and he felt the guilt heavily in his heart. He had no desire for anyone to know the truth about him. For some reason though he remained connected to the language. He loved the language and even after all these years he would dream in Bayash and on the rare occasions that he had tried to pray he had prayed in his mother tongue. He had even written some poetry in Bayash when he had been afraid in the refugee camp in the early days when it seemed they might be attacked.

He walked past a Croat house where the people were cooking some meat on a grill. The smell brought back the memories of when he was a child in his village before he was fostered out. He remembered how some of the men had taken an old bicycle wheel and turned it into a rotisserie and had cooked chicken on it over an open fire. He smiled as he remembered.

It was though memories of his sister that caused him the greatest pain. He should have made sure she had work or supported her in some way. It was as if life just moved on and in his mind he just seemed to disconnect with the realities of who he was and that he had responsibilities.

He found himself aching for Marija. He needed her so much now and yet he realized that what he had to do he had to do alone. He had told her that he had grown up in a foster home but he just could not bring himself to say the dreaded words, I am a Gypsy. To be a gypsy in Croatia was like being a black person in the south in America in the 1950's. The hatred was not so much at the feeling level as it was a deeply ingrained belief system that excluded their having any intrinsic worth or value.

He was part of the group that was referred to as "They." They are lazy, they are dirty, they are always drunk, they need to get jobs, they can't be trusted with a job. The cycle was endless and there was no way that dignity could ever be allowed to exist in their own thinking about themselves.

## Jasmina, Darko and Milena

As he walked he realized he was now close to the village. He knew that people would be welcoming but that they would talk behind his back as soon as he was in his old house. The village was just a small cluster of homes surrounded by the cornfields. The corn now was fully grown and it seemed to look like an ocean that swayed ever so gently in the wind. In the midst of the ocean was his home, an island of lost and unwanted humanity and a place he was returning to in guilt and sorrow not joy.

There was a crowd of people surrounding his old house. The people would probably not recognize him now after all these years but they would know he was coming. The young man that was sent to him would have given a full and exaggerated account of their evening. His small flat would be described as a palace, his friends at the table would now be his servants who bowed to him before speaking. He would own at least two Mercedes cars that had their own chauffeurs.

The crowd was silent and just staring at him. They backed away as he walked to the house stumbling over each other as they made way for him to enter.

His mother lay in the coffin in the center of the room. There were now dozens of candles in their red and white plastic holders on the floor, on a chair and on a small table. He immediately smelt death.

His mother's body had neither been washed nor treated and the heat of the day was turning it into a foul smelling form. She lay, despite the heat, icy looking and stone like. Flies were everywhere and settled on the dead woman's lips and eyes seeking to extract some kind of moisture from the decay.

Slavitsa was sitting with her back towards him holding the old ladies dead hand. Darko whispered her name. "Slavitsa?"

She quietly turned and then stood up. She was wearing a green blouse and blue jeans. She had several tattoos of the home

made kind on both arms and her upper chest. She looked him in the eyes. " Darko?"
He nodded and then held out both arms to her and then received her in an embrace that only a brother and sister can produce. She held on to him tightly and then stood back.

She cupped his face in her hands. "You came home." He nodded again then motioned for her to sit down and he then pulled a chair beside her and held on to her hands with his own.

Slavitsa looked closely at her brother. She could see his ears and his neck were clean. There was a fresh smell of cologne and his clothes seemed to her as if they were being worn for the first time. An almost overwhelming sense of pride rose within her.

She smiled and then spoke. " You made it just in time. They will be coming for the funeral very soon now. I have paid for a band, she would have wanted that."

Darko smiled and then looked at his mother's body. Nearly all his memories of her were ones of her being drunk. She had been so irresponsible and the men she kept were all bad. He reached into his heart to try and find some feelings of love but could not.

He looked at the tattoos on his sister's arms. Different names of men were etched in a dark blue die as a testimony that she was carrying on the family tradition.

The crowd outside the house began to scuffle, which meant the cart and band had come for the procession to the graveyard. The band was made up of six men. All of them were overweight none of their uniforms fit them. They stood together but at a distance from the village people. It was a signal to them and the village that they were not of the same species.

A cart was pulled up which was nothing more than a plank of wood on an old set of wheels from a pram. The coffin was taken, nearly dropped then placed on the cart. A young boy was recruited to carry the cross at the front of the procession. Directly behind the coffin were Darko and Slavitsa as they represented the family on this march to the graveyard.

The band was in front of the coffin and the men began to play slow mournful brass march music. The whole village broke down into small groups and followed behind in a slow procession. They looked more like refugees who were tired fleeing some enemy as they walked to the place of supposed rest.

The graveyard was excessively ornate. Large tombs with statues with the departed immortalized in engraved pictures into the marble, gave the place an atmosphere of almost regal and deep history. Neatly manicured pathways between the graves gave way to quiet places of rest with benches dotted around to give the mourners a place of reflection and quiet.

At the far end of the graveyard was the Gypsy section. Unkempt, crowded unmarked graves were huddled together like a group of unwanted visitors. No marble just the odd broken wooden cross with a name that meant so much to those who loved them and yet so lost without dignity in this place of shame and injustice.

The band brought the procession to an end as the group gathered around an open dug grave. The young priest with a kind and compassionate face stood alone looking into the hole in the ground.


Darko and Slavitsa sat alone in the house. It was now dark and the village was quiet. They had cleaned out the candles and plastic flowers and were sitting on the only two chairs in the house by the only table. There was a bottle of wine on the table and two unmatching cups that they drank from. The quietness and the wine allowed them to slowly reacquaint with each other and hear the stories that made up the last years of their lives. It was as if their lives had been made up of layers, some of which were public and many of which were deeply private parts of their consciousness.

They were interrupted by the sound of a car pulling up in front of the house. The door opened and the headlights of the car blinded them other than for the silhouette of a man standing in the doorway. He closed the door and the room seemed to descend into darkness. It was the moneylender.

He reached out his hand and shook Darko's and with a sense of seemingly genuine concern offered his condolences to him for the death of his mother. Darko thanked him in reply. The moneylender then spoke.

" Sorry about your mother, may she rest in peace. Listen you have a good sister and she is looking after the repayments. Anyway, I just wanted to drop in and offer my condolences and remind your sister that the I need the money on Thursday."

Darko turned and looked at his sister who was looking at the ground. " OK I have to go, sorry about your mother, Slavitsa you look great, I will see you on Thursday."

Once again they were blinded as he opened the door and the burning light from car headlamps poured in. As he left and closed the door there was a distinct sense of evil departing, as their eyes grew accustomed to the dark room.

As they sat down Darko poured wine into both their glasses and spoke. " Why don't you just tell me everything?" Slavitsa drank from the glass and then reached into her purse for a cigarette.

" Mama borrowed money to give to one of here boyfriends who wanted to buy an old beat up car. The car broke down, the boyfriend left and we were left with the loan."

Darko also drank his wine but he began to sense that with each drop of wine he was drinking he was partaking in an exercise of folly that had deluded millions of lives down through the years. He looked compassionately at his sister. " How much do you still owe?" She answered. " The same as when we borrowed it. We have

## Jasmina, Darko and Milena

just been paying the interest, which is 50% a month. You know how it goes."

Darko held his glass looking into its empty space. " How are you able to pay it off, you don't get any social for having kids?" Slavitsa looked at her brother and realized that it was no use hiding anything from him. Someone in the village would tell him about her soon enough anyway.

She spoke slowly. " I have to do a little bit of prostitution over the border in Hungary." Darko looked deeply into his sister's eyes. " How often do you have to work?" She looked down. " Every day, these are bad people Darko they have threatened to kill me and even you if I don't give them the money."

Darko stood up and went to the window and looked out into the village. This is why he wanted to be set apart from this culture and the constant drama of madness that everyday seemed to bring. He remained calm as he unpacked all that he had heard and seen but he felt a rage growing inside of him that right now was focused on the money lender but was in reality anger with and towards the whole world and perhaps even God for letting places like this exist.

He turned and reached out to his sister who seemed to collapse her tired form into his strong arms. " Listen to me, I will take care of the money but you are to finish with the streets, I will support you and care for you but you have to leave that life behind you, do you understand?"

Before she could reply there was a knock on the door. Bayash people almost never knock and so they both looked at each other with confusion. Slavitsa opened the door. Jasmina and Marija were standing in the shadows.

# 4
## Together

Ivan looked at the small hand made map that Jasmina had drawn for him. He could see that from her village, which had now been completely demolished, there was a path that crossed a small stream and that led into a thickly wooded area. It was along this path that Stefan had carried his precious wife after she had been beaten and abused by those who had invaded their village. Then there was a small clearing just about 50 meters from the stream. The map had an almost extraordinary exactness to it for something that had been drawn from memory.

He found the clearing and his heart sank as there were numerous trees around him and it was at this point that Jasmina's memory had faltered and she could not remember any particular direction that Stefan had gone to hide his cross in one of the trees. It was getting late and he needed to go back to the town where there was a Pension where he would sleep.

The ravages of war were still everywhere to be seen with buildings that had once been places of home or work now empty shells where just the sad ghosts of the past dwelt. He found within himself little or no bitterness to the Serbs as a whole but rather towards the ones who had harmed his beautiful young wife. When he wrote in the small journal that he was keeping, the night before, he was shocked at how he had written that the Serbs were by nature so much more open and friendly than his own people. Even as he had written, "his own people" he realized how he had allowed the prejudice of propaganda to infiltrate his mind.

## Jasmina, Darko and Milena

There was no such creature as a Croat he had decided. He smiled to himself as he thought of his Dalmatian friends who were as Croat as he was in their fierce nationalism but they were as different as him as it was possible to be in terms of genetics and emotional structure.

He had wrestled with this in his mind as he loved a Bosnian, but she was a Roma Bosnian, but she was also an Arli Roma Bosnian, which is so different from a Kalderash Bosnian Roma. He and Jasmina had decided that they would teach their children that labels were not of any great value and that as people they would be judged by God not according to their skin, language or religion but by the relationship they had with Him and how they loved and served others, even their enemies.

As he jumped across the small stream he stopped and looked at what used to be the village. All the ruins had been bulldozed away and it was now just an empty space. He wondered at the atmosphere. He had been thinking that it would have a sense of evil as if the demons that had laughed at the slaughter would still linger to haunt people such as himself that would come again into this space where evil was allowed free reign to express itself.

He could not feel evil but rather the absence of anything at all. It had reminded him of when he was at the Jasenovac death camps, there was the same empty feeling of nothingness that seemed to hang in the air.

Instinctively, he knelt down to pray and be quiet. His mind was silent. He found himself beginning to weep. He could not describe what in particular he was weeping for but rather he was overwhelmed by the sense of sadness and horror that people created in God's image could despise each other so deeply.

Darkness began to slowly descend and he felt no fear just a sense of awe. He got up from his knees and looked once more at the emptiness and started to walk towards the main road back to the town. It was getting dark and he needed to be fresh in the morning to search more for the cross and chain and also to investigate where his beloved Jasmina's family's graves were.

Marija and Jasmina sat on the bed whilst Slavitsa and Darko sat on the chairs. Marija was overwhelmed with what she felt, heard and saw. She like the majority of Croats had never been in a Roma village before. She had various images in her mind what it would be like but nothing could prepare her for this sense of being totally out of control and more like a tourist that a fellow citizen.

Darko spoke first. " Where is Stefan and where is Ivan?" Marija replied. " Stefan is at my parents but he will be going into hospital for more tests so I must get back tomorrow and then I will come and go as you need me."

Jasmina then spoke. " Ivan has gone to Bosnia for a few days so I can stay here and help in any way that I can. I can sleep here in this room." Jasmina was fully at ease. She looked across the room at Slavitsa and loved her. She noticed a skin sore on her neck that caused her concern but it was too soon to ask her about it.

Darko put his head in is hands. " I really don't deserve any of this but I am happy. I found my sister that I lost and then you…" He motioned at Marija and then quietly wept. A strange moment occurred that was hard for both Marija and Slavitsa as they both instinctively stood and came to Darko and tried to comfort him. They smiled at each other as the nurture rose within them both.

There was quietness and then a relaxing of the atmosphere. Darko spoke and explained to his sister that he had hidden his identity and how he was ashamed in front of Marija to be known as a Roma.

## Jasmina, Darko and Milena

Slavitsa laughed and then spoke. " You are acting like a Croat for having guilt about it. I would pretend to be someone else if I could but…" She showed the home made tattoos on her arms and laughed. " But it is obvious who and what I am." She smiled at the girls and continued. " You have to understand for us truth is not like it is for you, if we tell the truth it will be used against us, so we tend to use the truth in small doses ."

Marija wanted to interrupt and say that if you were going to marry someone the truth is important but she kept quiet. This was a whole new world that she had entered and her mind was racing in all directions.

Jasmina changed the subject. " Darko, why don't you take Marija for a walk around the village and Slavitsa and I can talk Ciganka to Ciganka."

The village was in fact quiet partly as a sign of respect for the death and partly as the evening was settling in and families were getting ready for bed. As they walked Marija felt herself relaxing. Darko then spoke. " I am very, very sorry for not sharing all this with you, but I want you to know that there is nothing more about me that is hidden or secret. I don't want you to be afraid that I am a person who would hide things from you." Marija nodded. He continued. " I realize how much I do love you Marija and how much I want to be your husband and be a father to Stefan. The truth is, I can not live without you."

Marija stopped and looked deep into his eyes. She knew at that inner intuitive level that he was telling the truth. She whispered in a voice shaking with emotion. " And I can not live without you." They suddenly clasped and held each other close in the silence of the night.

Jasmina smiled at Slavitsa and then spoke gently. " You are a prostitute I think?" The straightforward talk would have been offensive in other situations but for these women it was not.
" Yes, how did you know?" Jasmina looked at her new friend.
" God told me in my heart when we were sitting here earlier." Slavitsa shuddered. " Do you have a spirit in you that can read peoples minds?" Jasmina smiled. I have a spirit but not like the Vrachalala people. It is God's Spirit and sometimes He speaks so clearly to me and tonight He did."
There was a pause and then Slavitsa spoke. " I am going to give up the game as my brother is going to take care of our debts and look after me from now on." Jasmina smiled. " Your brother is my husband's best friend."

Slavitsa sat back relaxed and happy to have found a new friend. " Do you have family in any of the villages around here? But you are not Bayash I knew straight away."
" My Father, Mother, brother and sister were all killed in the war. I met your brother and my husband in a refugee camp." Slavitsa eyes widened. " Everyone dead. You must curse the people who killed them every day that their skin would fall from their bones." Jasmina looked to the side and then straight into Slavitsa's eyes. " No I don't. God has given me a peace that allows me to be quiet in my heart. I actually have forgiven them for what they have done." Slavitsa shuddered again. " I could not."

Jasmina was silent as if remembering and then spoke.
" Slavitsa, I have noticed that sore on your neck. How long has it been there?" Slavitsa reached to the spot then spoke. " A long time, I just ignore it" Jasmina responded. " I do not like the look of it and would like you to come with me to the doctor tomorrow"

The door opened and Darko and Marija walked in hand

## Jasmina, Darko and Milena

in hand. Darko spoke. " Marija is going back to Zagreb. You are welcome to stay Jasmina but…" Jasmina nodded then spoke. " Thank you, I will stay as Slavitsa and I have some things to do tomorrow together."

# 5
## News

Ivan sat on the ground in the graveyard. Under other circumstances he would have felt as if he were being disrespectful but in this case it was that he was simply overwhelmed. He had met an elderly man, Mr. Djokovich, the night before when he was walking home and somehow they had begun a conversation about what he was doing in the town and the fact that he was married to Jasmina. Astonishingly, the man had known her family and also Stefan's family and he had agreed to meet Ivan and show him where the graveyard was that had Jasmina's family's grave.

Thrilled that God had somehow intervened Ivan had gone with the man in the morning but not to one of the main graveyards but down a small dirt road and behind a field. There was an area that was enclosed by a fence but no religious symbols were to be seen. Mr. Djokovich pointed into the area and then agreed that he should leave Ivan to be alone to look for the graves and be quiet and reflective.

Everything was overgrown and in disarray. Ivan looked around and then began to try and uncover the small metal plates that were roughly embedded in cement. At first he thought he was in the wrong place as some of the plates had dates from 1941.

As he began to uncover more he realized what he had stumbled onto. This was a place where people who had been killed not just in the last conflict but also from the Second World War. They had been buried in some kind of secular manner. For some reason the local people had chosen to bury the recent victims of the war in the same space. It made no sense to him. Surely the different religious groups would want their people to be buried in their own sacred spaces not just thrown together in this pile. He brushed away dirt and weeds from plate after plate until he came across what he was looking for. Jasmina's father, mother and brother's names were all listed on the plate. He wept.

He cleaned the space but there was not much that could be done to give dignity to this resting place. He agonized as he thought of this family dying in suffering and not knowing about Jesus. He could barely face the issue and he cried out to God to help him make sense of what was without logic in his mind. He wondered why Jasmina's sister was not listed on the plate and reasoned that it was just a mistake or they did not find her body. He decided that he would come back later in the day after he had purchased some tools and spend the rest of the time cleaning up the area and praying over the place.

Jasmina opened her eyes just as the rooster, that seemed to be standing next to her, gave instruction that the time had come to start the day. She looked around the room. In one corner Darko was sleeping bundled in a large blanket. Lying on the floor on top of a coat was Slavitsa. Jasmina looked at her. She seemed so innocent as she slept. She thought of how her life must have been as a child growing up in such a place. She reached into her purse and took out her small pocket Bible. She read, as she did every day, three chapters of the Bible in order so that she could read through the whole Bible in about a year.

Closing her eyes she sang some songs in her heart without making any sound and then drifted into a conversation with God about all the things on her mind. She then prayed for Ivan and his parents, for Marija and Darko and Stefan and then prayed for Slavitsa that God would show her more things in her heart about her today. As she finished praying she turned once again to her Bible but this time to the back pages where she had written out a special set of words. Ivan had taught them to her and every day they would say them together. They started ' I believe in one God, Father almighty, the creator of heaven and earth'.

Ivan had taught her that love was the highest experience but love had to be fixed in truth and these words were the truth of God as found in the Bible. The rooster came again to give instruction and eventually all three of the friends were seated on either the bed or on the two chairs drinking coffee that was brewed Turkish style in a small pot with a long handle on the wood stove.

Stefan lay in the hospital bed with Marija sitting next to him. The tests had been completed and they were now waiting for the results. Stefan who had learned to sign as a means of speech shared with his adopted mother how he was afraid to change as he was now comfortable with himself and he did not know how people would treat him if he were ever able to speak.
" If you ever speak or if you live your life as you are now, the important thing to remember is that you are loved as you are. Darko loves you and wants to be a father to you. I love you so much it hurts." Tears welled up in her eyes as she spoke. " You have Jasmina and Ivan and so many others who love you."

As she was speaking the same young doctor who had been so friendly came up to them and pulled up a chair. He had some notes in his hand that he browsed over.

He smiled and then ruffled Stefan's hair. " Are you ready for some important news? Well, her we go. You have a growth or a tumor in your mouth that spreads down into your throat. It has probably been there since you were a baby. It is benign, that means we have done some tests to see if it is like cancer and it is not. It is just one of those things we cannot explain it is simply there. We can remove the tumor and if we do, we all agree there is reason to believe that after a lot of therapy you will be able talk normally."

Both Marija and Stefan were stunned. Without hesitation Stefan reached out to his new mother and then burst into a convulsion of tears. Marija too was crying but seemed to somehow connect her emotions to all that she had been going through and the result was an intense release of emotion.

The doctor smiled. " I thought it was good news and you are both crying. We can leave the tumor there if you like." He laughed. "Just joking, this is good news, very good news for you both. Anyway we do not need to rush this and this is going to take a few weeks to line up so go back to normal but look forward to the future."

Ivan sat in the coffee shop with Mr. Djokovich. There were more questions than answers rushing through his mind as he tried to process the information that had come into his mind that day. The old man spoke.

" I hope and pray to God that your generation will do something different about the future. I am Orthodox but I don't go to the church any more, just at Easter. I think if God wanted me to be involved with religion he would not have let me be born into this place. He can't expect anything more."

Ivan smiled one of those smiles that was neither an agreement nor a rebuke but rather a look of compassion and then drank from his coffee. and then responded. " Well, thankfully it is not so much what we do for God but what He does for us that is the key." He smiled and continued. " I want to thank you for showing me the burial place. It is strange though that the bodies were not moved to other places to be buried like the Muslims to a Muslim

## The Roma Chronicles

graveyard. There has to be one near here."

The old man looked away then replied. " I know but it was crazy here. When Arkan's crowd, may they rot in hell, came through there was not much left. They had their fun. They raped, killed, got drunk ate all the pork in sight and then moved on. We were left to pick up the pieces and someone felt it best just to bury people in that place. All the Muslims had gone anyway and their mosque and graveyard was destroyed. To be honest this was not a religious community here anyway. I don't think Selim ever went to the Mosque. "

Ivan felt the anger rising in his heart as the man talked of the carnage. The elderly man continued to speak. " So you are married to Selim's daughter Jasmina. He was a good man. He was educated you know. The other daughter what was her name, Semra I think, went mad when she found the family dead and her best friend cut up in their house. An hour earlier and she would have been dead to."

Ivan suddenly choked. " I am sorry I did not understand you. Jasmina's sister Semra was killed, murdered in the house."
" No it was another girl who was visiting. She came home after Arkan's lot moved on. She found her family dead and went mad. I think she is in a Mental Hospital now somewhere."

Ivan stood up and then sat down trying to control his emotions.
" You have to help me find where she is." The old man paused then spoke. " Let me think, I know, I am pretty sure she is in Banja Luka. We can call tomorrow and find out. I am sure she is in that NATO funded Mental Hospital."

Ivan sat down trembling all over. He whispered in his heart.
" Oh Lord Jesus Semra is alive, how can explain this to Jasmina."

# 6
## Given and Taken

Jasmina and Slavitsa sat outside at a café near the hospital. There was no one else sitting near them and their silence, which would have made people nervous normally, was comforting to them both. Slavitsa smoked a cigarette slowly and deliberately as if it were her last. She seemed to concentrate on each inhaling of the smoke as if it were a friend.

Jasmina spoke first. " I am so very, very sorry. How do you feel?"

Tears welled up in Slavitsa's eyes as she spoke softly. " I have been feeling numb but now I have this panicky feeling inside like I want to scream and run away somewhere."

Jasmina reached out and held her hand. Slavitsa drew again on her cigarette and then continued. " It is because I have sinned and God is going to kill me for my sins. I knew something like this would happen."

Jasmina squeezed her hand again. " I don't know how to respond to that Slavitsa. I do know this though that God will take you into His love if you are willing and He will care for you as a father."

Slavitsa sneered slightly. " Father is not the best example to use. My father started touching me in a bad way when I was about 8 years old."

Jasmina's face seemed to flush. " God is not like an earthly father but a heavenly one. He can only do good and what is right."

Slavitsa seemed to ignore the words but spoke. " If it had been just HIV positive then it would be one thing but they said it is full blown AIDS and there is nothing they can do. How could it get like this without me knowing?" She looked away then continued. " I thought I might have something to live for now that Darko has come back into my life and I can give up the streets. But there is nothing for me now just to rot away and die alone."

Jasmina could contain herself no longer and started to weep. Through her tears she stuttered a response. " You are not going to die alone. We will surround you with love. I will love you as my own sister like the one that was murdered. I will love you as if you were her. You and I will be sisters from now on no matter what happens."

Slavitsa started to cry also and Jasmina stood up and embraced her tightly. " Do you really mean that, I mean be my sister? I'm scared Jasmina. I am really scared. I don't want to die." Jasmina stoked her face then spoke. " I know, I know but we will carry you to God's garden in love, you will not be alone."

As she said the words she realized that something spiritual had transacted. This broken woman would be taken lovingly and gently to a father who knows all and would cleanse all the sin that had entered her young life.


Darko and Marija sat with Stefan at Marija's flat. Darko was there for the day but decided he would go back to the village in the evening to be with Jasmina and Slavitsa. He smiled at Stefan. The last days had wrenched from within him the need to constantly be joking and looking at life from a distance. It was a crisis that had created a process within him that he could already see had fundamentally changed his life. He spoke softly to Stefan. " It is great news about the medical situation." Stefan nodded and smiled.
Darko reached out to Marija's hand and held it gently. " Stefan, I have grown to love you as my own son. I loved you when I first saw

*Jasmina, Darko and Milena*

you back there in the camp with Jasmina but as the time has now gone by I have grown to love you and care about you deeply." He paused and looked down at the table and moved a cup from one hand to another before continuing. " Marija has agreed to marry me but we want to talk to you about it as it would mean we would live together as a family and I would be your Dad if you would let me."

Stefan sat still, looked at them both and then closed his eyes. He then rose from the table and went to his bedroom. There was no sound in the room just the slight and distant hum of the city coming from the background. Marija and Darko looked at each other in dismay. Darko thought it must be hard for the young man, as he had now become so attached to Marija that it would be hard for him to share her with anyone else. Marija was going to go the room but Darko touched her arm and motioned for her to wait. They were both silent looking at each other with a questioning look.

Stefan returned holding his pipe. He reached out and touched Marija on the face and then did the same to Darko. He put the pipe to his lips and then released spontaneously a joyous song. As he played he built up more and more into a free and joyful spirit. His eyes were closed and he swayed from side to side. As he finished he reached forward and kissed Marija on the forehead and threw his arms around Darko. Reaching into his pocket he took a piece of paper and laid it down on the table. On it was written " Mama and Papa" with a little smiley face. He smiled and took his pipe again and played his joyous song.


Ivan was in a kneeling position on the ground with a small shovel and was cleaning the graves one by one. His mind was reeling. There were so many conflicting emotions. Semra was alive and he would find out later today where she was and here he was now in an unofficial graveyard cleaning little markers that represented lives that had died in innocence. It hurt his back to bend in the way that he was and he realized that he had become out of shape since being married. He cleaned around each of the metal plates that were embedded in small concrete foundations. The names told him so much of what was going on. Jews and Serb names were the main ones. He felt sick inside. He realized that the recent killing and brutality had allowed for his own nationalistic conscience to be purged from his own people's history. It was as if the current conflict had been penance for the sins of the past and they were now free to hate without responsibility.

# 7
## Semra

Ivan walked into the psychiatric hospital that was run by NATO staff in Banja Luka. The building had previously been a school and was surrounded by nice gardens and it had a tranquil atmosphere to it. There was a security gate that surrounded the whole property that reminded the visitor that this was a place where people could harm themselves and others.

He walked up the stairs to the reception with his mind flooded with conflicting thoughts. He had seen in the camp young girls who had lost their minds due to the war. They were either completely lost and passive, usually because of medication or they were wild and almost terrifying to be around. He wondered how he would find Semra. In some ways he hoped she would be passive and detached. The idea of trying to take someone home who was violent and aggressive was frightening to think about. He was especially protective of how Jasmina would feel.

He entered into the director's office and introduced himself as a social worker and explained his story. The director, a man in is early 40's was warm and compassionate as they spoke. " Well, this case is a good news story actually." Ivan found himself guarded as he listened. The director continued and told Semra's story. " When she came here she was very distraught and depressed and potentially suicidal. She had arrived at the scene of the death of her family and her best friend. She was also terrified that her sister, your wife, had been taken away to one of the rape camps." Ivan interrupted. " But we listed this family with the Red Cross and the Red Crescent somehow the paperwork should have caught up with who was alive and who was dead and where they were."

The director smiled compassionately. " In principle, but this region was not an easy place to put together in terms of the facts. You had Serbs killing Muslims, Muslims killing Serbs, Croats killing and cleansing both Muslims and Serbs. I think they just wanted to move on and patch it up without too much investigation."

Ivan leaned back in his chair and looked at the ceiling. The director continued. " Well, Semra was actually in short term trauma and for some reason started to cope and fight back." He smiled and paused.
" Maybe someone was praying for her. The truth is she is fragile but not in any real need of being here. It is just that she had nowhere to go, and just between us, white coat to white coat, I have got quite a big budget so I actually ended up just keeping her on the books. She has her own little room and she actually helps out in my office. The truth is I will hate to see her go."

Ivan was overwhelmed with both relief and gratitude. He liked the director. " How should we do this? She can come back with me if we can do the paperwork." The director smiled. " The paperwork is no problem. I have the right of transfer through the Red Cross. She will have a UN pass and a Croat visa. When she is there you will have to figure out how to work through your end but there should be no big issues involved."
He laughed and then continued. " Whatever our differences as Serbs and Croats we have something in common that binds us, our need for unnecessary bureaucracy."

Ivan laughed but he wanted to cry. He wanted to call Jasmina but he knew he had to think things through very carefully. " When can I see her?"

## Jasmina, Darko and Milena

Darko held Slavitsa in his arms. The light was going down and as they stood in the small house in the village alone. They were aware that something precious was being given to them and being taken away at the same time. Jasmina and Marija had taken a walk outside to allow Darko and Slavitsa to be alone together. Darko stroked his sister's hair as he held her.

" My heart is breaking. I have just found you and now, if what they say is true I am going to lose you." Slavitsa stood quietly and then spoke.

" What happens when we die? I mean when I breathe my last breath what is going to happen to me? Will, I go somewhere as a spirit?"

Darko squeezed her tightly. " Jasmina and Ivan are the ones to help us with those questions. Let's sit down and go over this again and then I will make some phone calls to the doctors and see what can be done."

Slavitsa sat down and shared the story. She had AIDS but also some infections in her lungs that had spread to her liver that were actually untreatable and it was this that was going to kill her and it could be soon that she would die.

She was slowly getting used to telling the story and then suddenly changed the subject. " Tomorrow is Thursday and I have to pay the Kamata." Darko nodded and then spoke. " I will go over and see him and pay it all off. You can then forget about it all together."

Slavitsa then switched again. " I need to tell Angela, she is my friend in Hungary. She needs to tell my regular customers that I will not be coming back any more."

Darko sighed in a sad and sorrowful way. His sister was a prostitute but she was like a little girl. She was now more concerned about the filthy adulterous men who used her than her own desperate condition.

" Sure, we can call Angela and she can straighten everything out."

Semra was sitting on a couch in a small reception room when Ivan and the director walked in. She immediately stood up as a sign of respect. She was, Ivan thought to himself, so different looking from Jasmina but she had the same jaw and eyes. She was short and slender with long dark brown hair with just a tint of Jasmina's auburn. Her eyes also brown were wide and open almost child like or like a young deer. She smiled in a way that had a disarming charm and she was obviously still fragile and yet somehow able to fight on in her life. The two men sat down.
The director spoke first. " This is Ivan and he has some very good news for you so do not be worried or afraid." She smiled with relief. " I thought for a moment you would make me leave here. I don't have anyone and I have nowhere to go."

Ivan smiled gently and then spoke softly. He wanted to slowly unpack the layers of information in a way that would not cause her to go into shock. " I was working in one of the camps where people from your village came. I have some good news. Do you remember Stefan Petrovic? Well he is alive and safe."

Semra looked deeply into Ivan's face. He had a nice face she thought to herself there was something about him that made her feel she could trust him. " That is wonderful. I thought he was killed with his parents. That is wonderful. Can you tell me everything about him where he is and what he is doing."

Ivan smiled and then gently spoke again. " I will tell you everything, but I have some other news first. It is good news so don't be afraid." He wanted to reach out and say I am your brother and I love you because of Jasmina but he could not.

" This is going to be a shock, but Semra, your sister Jasmina is alive and well and living in Zagreb."

## Jasmina, Darko and Milena

There was a sudden thud as Semra fainted and fell forward to the floor. The windows were open and the Director got a glass of cold water. Semra revived and then started to cry hysterically. Both men were trained for these circumstances and they gently encouraged her as she began to unleash all the inward pain that she had no idea was still locked away inside of her.

Ivan then slowly began to tell her the whole story and that Jasmina had no idea that she was alive. He explained he was Jasmina's husband and that he had come to care for the family graves and had then discovered that she was alive.

He then told her that she could leave the hospital and come and live with them and that together they would help her just like Jasmina to have a completely new life. Within in a short time she was weeping softly giving way occasionally to laughter. Healing had begun.

# 8
## Violence

Slavitsa was lying down on the bed with Jasmina, Darko and Marija sitting beside her. It was as if the news that she was dying had taken away from her the will to live and she found herself becoming weaker in spirit and in body. The conversation as it often does at times like this turned to what would happen when death finally comes. Jasmina had now become the source for explaining these things.

" If Ivan was here he could help me explain things a little better." Slavitsa reached out her hand. " Don't misunderstand me, and I am sorry for saying it like this, but I am glad it is a woman who is helping me understand things."

Everyone understood and said nothing in reply. Jasmina continued. " The Bible says there is a heaven where there is no pain, sorrow or even sin only joy." Slavitsa looked at her then spoke softly. " But I am going to hell, because I have been so bad." Jasmina sat quietly praying in her heart.
" Let me explain things a little bit more."

She was just about to continue when there was ringing sound. It was Slavitsa's cell phone but rather than disturbing her Darko took and answered it. It was the moneylender. Darko felt a flush of both anger and hatred well up within him. He did not allow it show in his voice as he spoke in a detached way. In his heart he raged at this man who had threatened to kill Slavitsa and himself.

" OK, I will come over there now and meet you and we can work things out." He closed the flip phone, smiled at Slavitsa and

*Jasmina, Darko and Milena*

then explained that he must leave them to clear up the situation with the moneylender. Marija spoke. " I would like to come along and see how this works and just be there with you." Darko nodded his head. " I don't think you should as some of these people are not very nice." Marija was insistent. " I really think I should come, after all I am marrying into all of this." She stood up before he could answer and walked towards the door. " Anyway it is my car." She smiled playfully as she spoke.

Ivan walked back across the field, leapt over the small stream and headed back to where the clearing was. He had found Jasmina's family and tried as best as he could to clean the grave. He had found his sister in law and it seemed highly possible he would be able to take her home where she could be cared for and fully healed. He wanted to find the cross and chain and he also wanted to find the graves of Stefan's parents but he could not stay on indefinitely. He also had to think through carefully how he would explain about Semra being alive as the shock to Jasmina would be so great.

He arrived at the clearing and looked around. There had to be a method to his searching. He would estimate how tall Stefan was and what kind of place he would seek to hide the cross and chain. Carefully he planned out a strategy for covering the whole area without missing anywhere. He prayed as he walked and searched that God would somehow show him where to look.

Jasmina and Slavitsa were now alone. The room had a quiet and peaceful feel to it. " Slavitsa, let me try and explain what the Bible says about all these things, but let me pray first for you." Slavitsa nodded. Her heart was as open as it could be and she was desperate for some kind of spiritual comfort. " Jesus, you came to me in a dream, but you have not shown yourself to Slavitsa in the same way. Can you please open Slavitsa's heart so she can see how you feel about her and what you want to give her."

Slavitsa looked on amazed. " You talked to him like he was sitting here with us." Jasmina smiled. " He is, He is. But let me explain. God has given us laws to live by, you probably remember them from school." " Sure, don't kill, steal or take what is not yours." Jasmina continued. " Exactly, but there is more than that. We must love God with all our heart. We must not have anything or anyone else in our lives that is more important than Him, we must not even desire in our minds to have something or someone that is not ours." Slavitsa nodded." Well, that is why I am going to hell, I break God's law every day." Jasmina carried on. " The question is what does God do with people who break His laws especially when you realize that everyone has broken Gods laws. What should He do?" Slavitsa shrugged as if to say that she did not know. " Well he could let everyone go free. If he did it would be like a Judge in a court setting free people every time they came into court. He could not do that and be good."

Slavitsa propped herself up on her elbow and seemed to move closer to Jasmina as she spoke. Jasmina continued. " If he does not let everyone go, should He just let some people off who did not do such bad things as some other people? If He did then He would be saying some sin is less bad than other sin. But He says in the Bible that all sin deserves judgment."

Slavitsa looked serious. " So we all go to hell?" Jasmina continued. " The Bible says God made a way of escape for people who had broken his laws if those people would receive that way of escape."

Slavitsa looked even more intently. " What must I do Jasmina? I am going to die very soon. What must I do?" Jasmina reached out and touched her arm and continued. " Jesus came to earth to be with us. To teach us how to live and show us the truth of God but he also came for another reason. God decided to allow Jesus to be judged and punished for our sin so that we could be forgiven of our sin."

Slavtisa lay back down and looked up at the ceiling. " So that is why Jesus died on the Cross, he took the punishment for my sins. I always wondered why he did die like that." She lay still looking at the ceiling.
" Oh Jesus, I see it now. But even me? I am so dirty in my heart and body."

Jasmina sat still saying nothing as Slavitsa talked and reasoned with God. Then in the quietness she spoke softly. " Slavitsa I need to tell you something. I was raped in the war and horribly abused. You will say well that was not your fault and that is right. But "I" felt dirty and unclean. I felt so dirty I wanted to die. But actually my greatest sin was that I used the abuse I had received to pretend that I was not really a sinner. When I realized that I was overcome with how unclean I really was. Then I had a dream and Jesus spoke to me and told me I was pure and clean. Jesus died on the cross and poured out his blood so that you and me both dirty in our different ways could be clean and pure. Slavitsa if God forgives you and you receive it you are a virgin in his sight."

The words were too much for Slavitsa and she broke into weeping. As she shook she raised her voice to a shout almost bordering on a scream. " Jesus, I am so sorry, so sorry, make me clean please make me clean." She continued to talk to Jesus and then slowly she began to drift into a deep peaceful sleep.

# The Roma Chronicles

Marija pulled up outside the moneylender's house. It was a beautiful large newly refurbished property. The only houses that either of them had seen like this were in the nicer areas of Zagreb. The front garden had a swing and a highly ornate grill. There were white pillars at the entrance to a beautiful oak door.

Marija touched Darko's hand. " Don't do anything that we may regret afterwards." Darko hunched his shoulders. " Says she who nearly knocked down the Orthodox Church in Zagreb."

The door opened and the moneylender led them into a beautiful fully equipped kitchen and pointed to the chairs. He offered them coffee which they accepted.

" Thank you for coming. I am sorry about your mother and now I have just heard the news about your sister." Darko shook his head but was then waiting for the line about the money. He felt such contempt for the man and wanted to have an excuse to at least argue with him and perhaps even hit him.

The moneylender passed an envelope over to Darko who took it and looked inside. He looked at the man waiting for an explanation.

" That is all the money back that they have given me as interest. I have just kept the money that I loaned them in the first place."

Darko was expecting some kind of trick. Just as he was going to speak a young woman holding a baby came into the room. " This is my wife Marija and my daughter." Darko's Marija smiled. " Hallo, I am Marija as well." The woman smiled but was clearly shy.

Darko spoke quietly. " I don't understand, why are you doing this?" The moneylender began to appear moved emotionally. " I had a dream after I saw you the other night."

Without explaining the dream, which added to the mystery he

## Jasmina, Darko and Milena

continued. " I hate doing what I do. I have got rich from these peoples misery but they would borrow from someone else anyway. They never borrow money for anything important. It is always beer for parties, for name days or old cars that are going to crash or stupid things. Then I have to threaten them or they would never pay the money back."

Darko was stunned. Marija looked on in wonder. " When I saw you at the house the other night it made me think. This kid got out of here and has done something with his life. There was something about you and I told my wife about you. I drove home and I could not sleep. I just kept thinking that I was not made to hurt people and squeeze them for money. Then when I did go to sleep I had the dream."

Darko wanted to shout at the man to tell them what the dream was. The moneylender continued. " Anyway, I am done, finished and I am out of the Kamata business. There is something more. I was thinking maybe I could start a club for kids to learn how to mend engines or something. Just think, if we had people like you to become doctors and lawyers and then people like me to teach kids to have good jobs. Well, who knows what could happen. "

Darko was deeply moved. He thanked the man shook his hand was going to turn and leave then reached out and gave the man a hug. Marija kissed the wife on each cheek and then they left the house. As the car drove away they were both silent then Darko spoke. " This is going to sound crazy to you but for the first time in my life I am proud to be a Bayash Roma." Marija smiled. " Well if you think that is crazy, I was just thinking, I wish I was a Bayash Roma." Darko smiled and then laughed.
" Oh man I can't believe any of this happening. The other thing is I think God is trying to get our attention to be like Ivan and Jas.

You know really get into knowing Jesus." Marija smiled and then whispered. " Me too." She continued. " What do you think the dream was, that he had?" He smiled. " Maybe he saw a vision of you knocking down the Orthodox Church and thought I don't want to come against this woman as she is not be tangled with."

# 9
## Life and Death

The paperwork had been cleared up and Semra was free to leave with Ivan and go home with him to Zagreb. Ivan was disappointed that he could not find either the cross and chain or Stefan's parent's graves. Perhaps these were things that were just going to be a mystery like so much that happens in life.

He had decided to go back one last time to visit Jasmina's family's grave. He wanted to walk rather than drive and found himself praying as he went. The morning was fresh and warm but not oppressive. He had always loved the sounds of the birds singing and this morning their seemingly chaotic chorus was a delight to him.

He turned the corner to go up the small dirt road to the graveyard and heard the sound of voices. He slowed down to listen. His immediate reaction was that some people had come to desecrate the graves perhaps because the word had got around that a Croat was in the area looking at graves.

The type of conversation and the atmosphere itself betrayed something different was in the process of being performed. He walked from behind the trees and came to the fence. Mr. Djokovich was there with a group of men and women who were all in the process of cleaning and tidying the area. One man was laying concrete and some women were planting some small bushes. Mr. Djokovich came over to the fence to where Ivan was standing.

" We decided that we should be responsible for this little graveyard." Ivan was deeply moved and found it hard to speak without breaking down. " I don't know what to say, but thank you, thank you very much." Mr. Djokovich smiled. " Well, at times like this maybe it is best not to say anything. Hey, but let me tell you something. I went to the Church yesterday for the first time in a long time. It all seems smells and bells to me right now but maybe God will find me instead of me trying to find him."

Ivan nodded. " I don't know if we will meet again but I am gong to pray that God does find you and that when He does you will recognize it and be at peace in your heart." The old man smiled. " We all want peace, but I think something happened because you came here, I think I want to know God and what he wants for me to do with what is left of my life."

He pointed to the work going on at the graves. " I know this is the right thing to do." Ivan nodded and then reached out and shook his hand.

Both Marija and Darko ran from the car park up the steps and into the hospital. Then went straight to the children's surgical department. Stefan had had the surgery and was seemingly doing well. They had left a few hours before and decided to get some rest. The phone had rung at Marija's flat and she had called Darko immediately.

Stefan was reacting to something that the doctors did not know why and was now slipping away into death. The went straight into the doctors office and were seated.

The young doctor looked very concerned and was as compassionate has he could be. " I am afraid it is very bad news and you must prepare yourself for the reality that Stefan may not make it."

The words were like a knife thrusting deeply into Marija's

heart. She immediately broke down. " He is going to die, first my husband and then my baby and now my little boy. I can not take any more of this."

Darko said nothing but placed his arm around her. He turned to the doctor and then spoke. " Can we go and sit with him?"

The doctor led them through the light green sterile corridors to a room where Stefan was laying. A nurse was attending him. She looked at the doctor and shook her head and then left.

Stefan was a ghostly pale color. He had tubes coming out of his throat and had various instruments connected to his body. He was breathing in a shallow and slow manner.

The room itself had a feel of death to it. The lights were low. The sounds of the monitors gave more prominence to the machine than the living human being. There was a smell of disinfectant that gave the impression it was trying to mask the smell of death that hung in the air. Marija held Stefan's hand and laid her head on the bed resting close to him. Darko had his hand on her shoulder. He prayed out loud.
" God, I have tried to run from you all my life but now you are moving close to me. You are giving and taking all the time. I don't understand. But I do know that you are real. I know you are alive in Jasmina and Ivan and now even in poor Slavitsa. Be real to us Lord, help us Lord. Please don't let this little boy die, not like this." Marija lifted her head slightly. " Can you keep praying, it gives me comfort."

Slavitsa and Jasmina sat together in the room in Slavitsa's small house. Slavitsa was propped up in the bed and looking weak. Everyone had been so surprised how rapidly she had gone down and all the talk was that she was dying and would soon be dead. Jasmina was reading Psalm 23 to her. Slavitsa closed her eyes and spoke softly. " You know I am scared of dying but I am not afraid of death." Jasmina squeezed her hand. " Ivan says that it is natural for us to try and hold on to life as long as we can. God has made us that way. But when we cannot hold on any longer and we have to let go then God steps in and takes over. That is why you will be at peace when you go to heaven. You will go to sleep and then wake up in heaven."

" What is Ivan like? You adore him don't you?" Jasmina smiled. " I do. He is strong, he is good he is gentle and he is wise."

Slavitsa smiled in reply. " I guess any of us would adore someone like that. But there are not many like that. I think my brother is though, don't you?" Jasmina replied. " Yes I do and he and Marija are going to be very happy together."

Slavitsa smiled again and then looked into Jasmina's face. She was so good and pure. " I have never been loved by a man like that. I don't know what is to be protected and cared for." Jasmina reached out and stroked her head and then spoke. " When you go to heaven you will be loved by so many people. I think God is going to give you a special job in heaven."

Slavitsa looked up. " Tell me what do you think he would have me do in heaven." " Well, I can't say but I think when you get there you are going to discover all kinds of things. You will be able to sing, paint, sculpt, cook and do all kinds of things but like the greatest artists who have ever lived." Slavitsa sighed. " Oh Jas, I want to go there quickly now."

Jasmina reached out again and stroked her hair. " I know but God has given you to us for a little longer to enjoy being with. We all love you and you have become my sister."

## Jasmina, Darko and Milena

Ivan pulled up to the hospital in his car. Semra was standing on the steps with her small bag. The director was there with several staff members and also some of the patients. They were in a group around Semra and there was a genuine sense of both joy and sorrow that she was leaving.

The director shook hands with Ivan and handed him an envelope with documents inside. " Everything is there, she has her UN pass and the Red Cross visa is inside."

Ivan smiled and shook hands and then took Semra's bag and put it on the back seat of the car. The director reached out and gave her a big hug. She began to cry and then hugged all of the people with her. As the car drove away the people waved and followed until they were out of the gate and on the road.

Ivan looked across at her. " Are you going to be OK?" She nodded and then replied. " I am afraid of being away from the hospital but I can not even tell you what is going on inside about being able to be with Jasmina again. Does she know we are coming?"

Ivan laughed nervously. " Not yet, she is staying in a village near where we live but there is no phone there. She is helping my best friends sister who sadly is dying." Semra looked out of the window at the fields and the trees rushing by her. " What shall we do?"

" I am going to take you to my sisters flat and then I will go and get Jasmina and bring her down and explain to her that you have come. Then we can move over to our place and then, I will disappear while you two talk for as long as you need."

# 10

## The Pathway

Ivan and Darko stood alone in the corridor of the hospital. Darko leaned against the wall with his head pressing against it as he looked upwards at the ceiling. Marija had remained in the room with Stefan. Darko felt an overwhelming inward tension that was building up in his chest. He looked at Ivan and then spoke. " I have decided, actually Marija and I have decided that we are going to follow God and we want to learn to know what that means."

Ivan looked into his face with compassion but did not speak. Darko continued. " The truth is though I do not know how to deal with all of this at the same time. My mother dies, I find my sister and now she is dying. Stefan is dying and then you come back with Semra. It is almost too much to bear."

Ivan also felt the sense of being in a whirlpool and out of control. He braced himself and then spoke. " Well, let's try and deal with this one step at a time. I have taken Semra to my place. I was going to suggest that she stay with Marija but not now with all this uncertainty."

He was going to continue when a nurse came to them. She asked who Ivan was and then showed him into a room where there was a telephone. When he picked up the phone it was Semra's voice. He had given her the hospital number in the event of an emergency.

" Ivan, I am sorry to call you." There was a timid almost vulnerable manner to her way of speaking. " But Mr. Djokovich telephoned for you and said would you call him at his house as it is very important." Ivan reassured that she did the right thing to call him and then hung up.

## Jasmina, Darko and Milena

Darko was now sitting with his head in his hands when Ivan returned. " Listen I have to make a phone call but I will be back straight away."

He purchased a phone card and went to the public phone and called Mr. Djokovich. He hung up the phone after a brief call and ran back to where Darko was sitting.

" Listen this is all too complex to explain but I have got to go back to Bosnia now. I can do it in about 5 hours round trip. I have to go." Darko was left standing in the hospital corridor without having time to either react or to process what his friend was saying.

Marija sat close to Stefan and stroked his hair. From time to time he would come round into consciousness and then drift back again into a deep sleep. The doctor came into the room and then asked Marija and Darko to come to his office.

" The situation is this. He has some kind of infection that is affecting his liver and kidneys. We are using anti-biotics but so far there is little response. He is though holding his own right now. We need something that would cause him to kick into a fight back to save his own life. It is as if emotionally he is not fighting. I think it would be good for you both to talk with him even when he is asleep and try and motivate him." Darko thanked the doctor and both he and Marija went back to the room to start a long night of attending to him.

Semra walked around the flat. It was thrilling for her. She went into the kitchen and looked in all the draws. She was amazed at all the knives and forks and other utensils that Jasmina had. She looked into Ivan and Jasmina's bedroom. She felt a little guilty but could not resist the temptation to look through all of Jasmina's clothes. She would hold them to her face and smell them as if to draw closer to her sister.

She then sat down with the wedding photo album and wept as she saw her sister for the first time. She was just the same but with a deeper look of maturity to her face now. She wondered how she would fit in living in this flat and that perhaps one day she would find someone like Ivan who would love and protect her and give her, her own little flat where she could be a wife and mother.

But now this was joy and tomorrow she would see her sister again for the first time. She fell asleep in the chair and was at peace through the night until Ivan came into the flat in the early hours of the morning. She could hear him taking a shower and then he was off again out of the flat without saying a word.

Jasmina was sitting next to Slavitsa by the bed. Slavitsa was sleeping peacefully when there was a knock on the door. Jasmina opened the door and within a moment was in Ivan's arms weeping with both joy and sadness at all that was going on. Before he could say anything. She asked about Stefan.

" I want you to come with me if you can leave Darko's sister for a couple of hours. Is there anyone who can sit with her?"

" There is a lady, a good lady here in the village I will ask her. But I need you to meet Slavitsa first."

Jasmina gently stroked Slavitsa's face and whispered her name. At first she remained in her sleep and then slowly came round.
" Slavitsa this is Ivan."

Ivan reached out and took her hand in both of his and smiled. " Your brother is my best friend, I am happy to meet you." Slavitsa was still sleepy but replied.

" Jasmina is my sister now. She is my special sister and also my sister

## Jasmina, Darko and Milena

in Jesus." Ivan smiled with kindness. "That is wonderful Slavitsa wonderful."

The lady from the village came to sit with Slavitsa as the couple got in the car and drove off. Jasmina leaned against him as he drove. She loved his smell as much as she loved to look at him. He smiled and then spoke as he drove. " Darling this is going to be a very emotional time for you."

" I know, is it really true that Stefan will die?" He looked ahead at the road as he spoke. " Well, we are working on that and it is important that we all be there for him right now. But there is something else."

He pulled the car over into a lay by. He turned the engine off and then reached across to hold his wife tightly in is arms. " What is it Ivan, has something terrible has happened, is it your parents?" He continued to hold her tightly. " There is something wonderful, wonderful news. Your sister Semra was not killed and she is alive."

Jasmina thought she would pass out. She pulled away from Ivan and looked into his face. She felt numbness. The kind of numbness that she had experienced at the time of the war. " Semra, alive?" At that point she burst into almost hysterical weeping and held tightly onto Ivan pulling him closer and closer as if trying to hide herself within him.

Marija and Darko went once more into the doctor's office. He was a kind man for someone so young and seemed to exude a trust that people could draw strength from.

He spoke before they sat down. " OK well this is the situation. He is stable. That is he is not out of danger but he is holding his own. I think it is good that you are talking to him. This also could be related to the fact that he has gone through enormous emotional trauma and that the surgery may have actually stimulated some deep fears of change. I don't know to be honest but we need something to boost him inwardly to help his system fight the infection."

Marija looked so drawn and tired that the doctor spoke to Darko. " Look I think your wife needs some rest." Immediately Marija responded.
" No I am ok and I need to be with my son." The doctor continued addressing Darko. " I think you should work in shifts for a little while. You can use the extra bed in the room to take turns sleeping on."

# 11
## Sisters

The door to Ivan and Jasmina's flat opened. They decided they would just walk in and make themselves known to Semra. Jasmina could almost sense her sister was close by and the feelings that ran through her mind were both intoxicating and foreboding. She was at first outwardly calm and quietly closed the door but then found herself calling out Semra's name. Ivan had never seen his wife so excited. Semra appeared from the kitchen.

She was wearing a white sweater and green trousers. She gasped when she saw Jasmina standing before her. She stood for a moment and paused and looked at her sister that she loved so dearly and had believed was gone. It was as if time had been erased and they were back together as if parted only yesterday.

Jasmina's lips quivered as she looked at Semra. It was as if her mind was swimming and the whole scene was being acted out at a distance.

They both stood looking at each other almost rooted to the spot. Jasmina turned her head and looked out of the window and wondered if there was a white dove there. Ivan stood quietly praying in his heart.

Almost as if a match had ignited a patch of petrol the two sisters threw themselves into each other's arms and wept loudly. They both shook in convulsions of emotion.

Jasmina would draw back and look at her sister and then draw her to herself again crying out her name loudly. The tears from both of them mingled on each other's cheeks as they wept and kept saying each other's names.

Ivan stood and watched. He had never seen his wife be so dramatic and loud. He loved her. There was something beautiful taking place in that the pain of the loss they both had known and experienced was now being redeemed in some strange way.

Jasmina was the first to speak. " I can not believe this, I can not believe this I thought I had lost you forever."

Semra laughed and cried. " And I also thought you were dead. You just disappeared and were gone."

Jasmina began to remember the horror of that day. " Little Stefan Petrovich carried me into the woods and we were rescued and then we went to a camp and that is where I met Ivan."

Once more they began to weep and hold each other tightly. Ivan walked over to them and put his arms around them both. He spoke gently. "Come and sit down and I will make some coffee and you can both slowly adjust to what is happening."

Jasmina nodded and whispered her thanks to him. The sisters sat down still holding on to each other as Ivan went into the kitchen to make the drinks.

Jasmina spoke again to her sister. " I don't want you to ever leave me again." She looked at her sister and then stroked her face. " You must have suffered so much did you see Mama and Papa and Hamid when they were killed."

Semra looked down and then replied. " I still see them, and my friend Nada, every night when I try to sleep but the people at the hospital were very kind and they helped me with some ways of not crying all the time and how to deal with it."

Jasmina sighed. " Well, you are safe now and you can live with us forever or for as long as you want. Ivan is a good man."

" I know, he is so different isn't he. He is like one of those men in the movies."

Jasmina giggled and then held her sister again. " He is so

gentle and kind, he never gets angry with me and we are like best friends as well as man and wife. And it is a little strange for you to understand this now but we both love God and really have spiritual things as the most important part of our lives."

Semra smiled. " I knew he was religious by the way he spoke about things. It is funny though because we never had that in our home. I think in Mama a little bit but it felt like that was something for other people."

Jasmina looked sad as she began to think once more about her family. " Well, we can talk about it later but this home is a safe place and it is a pure place where love and trust are normal."
Ivan came back into the room with a tray of cups of coffee and some cakes. He placed it on the table and then served the two sisters. He stood leaning against the wall and watched his wife and new sister in law. He then spoke softly to them. " Stefan is not doing well and the doctors said it would be good if we could do something that would help increase his will to fight for his life. Can we go down to the hospital now? Then we can come back and eat and I will go to bed and you can talk and then we can decide what needs to be done with Darko's sister Slavitsa."


Stefan remained sleeping with just an occasional stirring. Darko sat on the bed next to Marija. He stroked her hair. " You are exhausted, I should have insisted that you rest, I am sorry." She kissed his hand. " You are tired too and now you have Stefan and Slavitsa to worry about." He smiled at her and realized how much he loved her. " You know, it sometimes takes pain and suffering like we have gone through to realize what is important. I am thinking about and talking to God all the time in my heart. It is like I am not quite there but I am definitely on some kind of journey, or you know it feels like lights are slowly turning on in my heart. But I realized how much I love you and need you and want to do whatever is needed to make your life full and happy."

He paused for a moment. " I have this strange feeling though. I think Stefan is going to be better but I know my sister is going to die."

Marija rested her head against his chest. " I am so sorry but you know I have the same sense that God is not going to take Stefan from us and that He, that is God is going to use Stefan in a special way."

Darko breathed out. " I am thinking of bringing my sister to my flat and let her die in a more comfortable place. Or if not I will move in up there until she dies and really make it a comfortable place for her. It is just I would like her to have a bathtub and a toilet for the first time in her life."

There was a gentle knock on the door. Ivan then opened the door and walked in. Ivan reached over and kissed his sister on the cheek and then gave Darko a hug. Darko spoke first. " Where did you go? You must have driven all night."

Ivan smiled. " I did but it was worth it. I have Jasmina and Jasmina's sister Semra. Let's bring them in and see if we can lift Stefan with their visit."

The two sisters walked in holding hands. Jasmina kissed Marija on each cheek and hugged Darko before whispering her introductions of her sister. The group then drew up chairs and quietly gathered around Stefan.

Jasmina stroked his head. " Stefan it's me Jasmina." He slowly opened his eyes. "My sister Semra is here she is alive she did not die."

His eyes widened and he seemed to rouse very slightly. Semra then spoke. " It is true Stefan, I am here."

Whatever the doctors had hoped for began to work as if

## Jasmina, Darko and Milena

by some magical process the spirit of the boy began to rouse. He looked around and saw Marija and Darko, Ivan and Jasmina and now dear Semra.

He started to move very slightly and looked at each person in the face. Ivan moved closer to him. He also stroked his head and then spoke quietly. " I have something for you."

He reached into his pocket and took out a small envelope. Then from the envelope he removed a silver cross and chain. He took Stefan's hand and put it in it. Stefan's grip tightened for the first time in days holding that which was so precious to him. Tears began to fill up in his eyes. He nodded and then smiled. The whole room seemed to be breathing in unison at his rebirth or rather as his re entry to life began to take form.

He looked at Marija and then at Darko. Then in a whisper uttered his first attempt at speech in his whole life. The words made little sense to those who did not know them but for all gathered the words were clear and precious. " Mama, Papa."

Marija burst into tears and held his head and kissed his forehead. Darko placed his arm around her. The two sisters held hands and Ivan felt satisfied and complete. It was dear old Mr. Djokovich who had taken all his fiends into the woods to look for the cross and chain and had called him with the news.

# 12

## Three Weeks Later

Slavitsa lay in a bed in the front room in Darko's flat. There was a small coffee table to the side of the bed. On the coffee table was a small dolls house, a cheap children's make up kit, a small teddy bear and a young girls note book or diary. There were a few beads and colored pencils as well as some children's books.

Darko had decided to surround Slavitsa with the things that were missing in her childhood. In these last days of her life she would be kept away from the pain of the world and live in a protected innocence provided by those who loved her.

She was becoming increasingly fragile and childlike and he wanted to surround her with childlike things. She was finding it almost impossible to eat now and so he had cut up little slices of grapefruit and laid them in a silver cup on a bed of ice. She loved to sip from it very slowly and just enjoy the tangy sensation of the grapefruit in her mouth.

She loved her brother so much and was so proud of him. She kept saying it was the right thing to do to leave the village but it was good that he was no longer running from being Bayash.

It was becoming clear that she would not live long now. In the evenings she would have him read the Bible to her and together they would say very simple prayers of both thanksgiving and then ask God to bless various people.

Often she would say that one day God would send someone to their people who would translate the Bible into Bayash so that they would be able to love the Word of God in their way. Darko had

## Jasmina, Darko and Milena

got clearance to take leave from his job for as long as he wanted to care for her and so he devoted his whole time to her care.

He had a sense that today was the day that Slavitsa would leave them and go to heaven. As he woke up he had a clear focus in his mind that he should have the others come over one last time to be with her as it was now very close to the end.

He and Marija had decided they would get married in a few weeks time. They were hoping Slavitsa would still be with them but it was obvious now that she could not move out of the apartment.

She loved staying there where it was always warm and she could use a proper toilet and also have a shower. Before she had got too weak to move she would have a shower sometimes three or four times a day. He purchased all kinds of creams and perfumes for her, which she loved to put on in the evenings.

Jasmina and Semra were the first to come and they came into the room holding some flowers that they neatly arranged on Slavitsa's special memories table. They sat down next to her. Semra massaged her feet whilst Jasmina gently stroked her head.

" You really are my sister now Jasmina." As she said the words she started to choke up. She was becoming very fragile emotionally.
" Yes, and I am proud to have you as my sister."
" Do you mean that?" Slavitsa looked deeply into her eyes.
" I love you as deeply as it is possible to love and I would be happy to tell the world you are my sister."
" Even though I have been such a sinner?"
" Especially because we have both been forgiven our sins."

The doorbell rang again and Marija and Stefan walked into the room. Stefan had healed so quickly and was now already speaking slowly and with simplicity.

Marija went to Darko and hugged him and then kissed him. She found it almost unbearable to see him suffer the broken heart of losing his sister but she was also inspired by him and the way that he was so in control and not letting the pain push him down.

Last to come was Ivan who had left work early to be with them. His kissed his sister, hugged Darko and then stood behind Jasmina and kissed her on the head. Slavitsa looked almost blissfully happy to be surrounded by memories and friends. She kept saying that she was bathed in peace and love. She spoke almost in a whisper.

" Ivan, you said I would have a new body in heaven, will it have the same tattoos that I have now?" Ivan reached over and squeezed her hand. " No Slavitsa, there will be no tattoos in heaven."

She looked serious. " I am glad, because these don't have good memories for me."

Jasmina spoke gently to her. " In heaven there will no bad memories at all. God has already forgotten all your sins and when you go to heaven you will forget them also."

" That is lovely, your words Jasmina always make me feel peaceful. Is Stefan here?"

Stefan came close sat down with her. His shirt was purposely open so that his cross and chain could be seen by all. He spoke in a hoarse way and a like a deaf person as it was taking time for him to learn to actually say words. " I want to play something for you on my pipe."

He took his pipe that had now traveled so far and through so many places. He began to play a song in a minor key but of such a manner that it had both joy and beauty to it. Slavitsa closed her eyes and began to gently sway her head to and fro. When he stopped there was an almost sacred feel to the room as if the music had called angels to come and share in this moment. Stefan spoke to her again. " This is my gift to you"

There was suddenly a change in the room as Slavitsa answered him in Bayash. She then started to speak more in Bayash.

## Jasmina, Darko and Milena

Everyone looked at Darko who then acknowledged that he should translate.

" She says that you all have bathed her in love and that she is now ready to go to heaven."

There was a pause and then it was as if Slavitsa's face lit up with a radiance that seemed otherworldly. She had an open smile of joy on her face as if she had seen a long lost friend. She was breathing heavily and looking as if she would get up from the bed and run towards whomever it was she was seeing.
She called out. " She says she can see Jesus" Darko's voice began to break as he translated. " She says he is standing right here in the room."
" She says." He broke down and Marija put arms around him. " She says, she says Jesus is speaking to her in Bayash. She says he is speaking in Bayash."

There was very briefly a glorious look of wonder on her face and then stillness. The room felt as if a great company of angels had been there and had now gone taking their beloved with them.

Darko knelt down before her and lifted her body into his arms. Her limp tattoo covered arms hung lifeless as he held her. Her face was peaceful and her eyes were closed of their own accord.
He spoke to her in the Bayash language of his love for her. He told her they had such a short time together but it was precious and he would treasure these moments forever. He then wept like a child as he rocked too and fro holding her body in his arms. Everyone was weeping unashamedly and holding each other in embraces of love and kindness.


No one had ever before experienced the power of love that comes from Jesus quite like this. There was an unutterable sense of peace in the room that no one wanted to leave. Jesus had been there and taken their Slavitsa to heaven. She was now at rest in a place where she would not remember her sins any more, her tatoos were no more and were Jesus speaks in the Bayash language.

Part Three

Milena

Everyone Can Forgive

And Be Forgiven

# 1
## The Curse

The room was both dark and foreboding. The blackness that could be felt or sensed was broken into by a small light in the corner. An old tin, once discarded but now reborn, was filled with animal fat. Resting in the midst of the fluid, which was once a pig, was a thin twig. The twig acting as a wick gave enough light to punctuate the darkness but not enough to erase the heavy blanket of despair that darkness so often carries with it.

Shrouded by the darkness yet revealed by the timid light was Yanchi Orshus sitting on a lone chair. He lent back with his head against the wall. His thick black hair was greasy, as if dipped in the same place that the light was coming from. Above his head, hung a picture of the Blessed Virgin. Next to the frame of the holy one was another female, less blessed and certainly not a virgin torn from the center spread of a magazine. Across the room on a single bed sat his brother Radovan. Both men made a contribution to the atmosphere by chain-smoking homemade cigarettes. Tobacco that had yesterday lain discarded in the street was now recycled to bring comfort in time of need.

Yanchi was in his early twenties, Radovan a few years older. He had a scar over his left eye, which had removed part of his eyebrow. Both men had homemade tattoos in both cases spelled incorrectly. Yanchi's eyes were black. Added to their color was a deep and dark stare that caused most onlookers to question his sanity.

Radovan, from the same father, but a different mother, had softer features and with a slight ginger tint to his mild brown hair.

## Jasmina, Darko and Milena

A door stood between the room in which they were seated and another smaller room. From this ominous chamber came the sounds of moaning that swelled into a crescendo that culminated into a cursing scream. Yanchi's wife, Irena, was giving birth to their child. Irena lay on a solitary bed in the otherwise empty room. Her sister, Smiljana, sat with her encouraging her by joining her voice to the curse that was coming from her lips every three minutes. Irena did not know how old she was but was about fifteen or sixteen years of age. Her long raven black hair was covered in sweat. As each set of contractions intensified the sisters turned their cursing to Yanchi and men in general.

Smiljana waited for a suitable interval and then opened the door and asked Yanchi where the ambulance was and why it was taking so long. Almost as if choreographed by a stage director the outside door opened and a young woman stood in the doorway. She offered no greeting just the news that the ambulance was at the edge of the village and that they were afraid to enter the village itself.

Irena screamed again and Smiljana joined her in cursing the ambulance and their own mother for bringing them into the world. Irena dragged to her feet and supported by the two brothers and her sister, made her way into the street. The distance was about 100 meters to the edge of the road where the ambulance was waiting.

The village was made up of about 20 small houses. Most of them were just single room dwellings while some had two rooms. The headman of the village had a large house with 6 rooms surrounded by a concrete wall. From his house the reflection of television could be seen from outside. None of the other houses had electricity or running water.

To go to the toilet was simple. The children went anywhere they liked, whereas the adults crouched behind the back wall of their tiny homes.

Tonight the single street that ran through the village was a sea of mud. Animal waste and that of the children found itself worked into the mud creating a slimy foul-smelling mass that Irena was dragged through.

In the distance a warm and consistent light could be seen in the form of the ambulance waiting as either a predator or a source of comfort on the edge of the village. Radovan held his sister-in-law with an unusual gentleness as Yanchi walked ahead. The tiny pinprick of light coming from his cigarette was like a guiding laser leading the pilgrims to their destination.

Smiljana called down a curse upon Yanchi in the form of a request that the skin would fall from his bones and that his blood would rot in his body. Yanchi slowed down and then slapped his sister-in-law in the face. She fell silent and Yanchi reached out his other hand and passed her a cigarette that he had been smoking.

The back door of the ambulance opened causing a wave of warmth and light to pour out onto the street bathing the curses and the cursed together in one great stream of confusion.

One of the medics reached out to help Irena into the ambulance. Radovan quickly whispered in Irena's ear, "If it is mine, you will know." Her tired contraction-racked body was lifted into the ambulance. A tall blond-haired medic with golden stubble on his chin turned to the group in the mud, "You are too dirty to come with her, you will have to make your own way down to the hospital."

The door closed before the paroxysms of hate could reply and in a moment the ambulance was driving away. Yanchi, Radovan and Smiljana stood alone in what was now almost complete darkness. Then from a shadow that had appeared as the moon wrestled itself free from the clouds could be seen an old woman.

She was holding an open bottle of beer in her hands. They were clasped around the body of the bottle as if holding the sacred cup at Mass. Her eyes were as dark as Yanchi's but with a mystical edge of evil about them. She drank from the bottle liturgically and

## Jasmina, Darko and Milena

then spoke. "The baby is cursed, you will see, there is no way out."

The cold words seemed to hang in the air as she turned and disappeared into the shadows where she seemed to belong. As she left a cold breeze rustled through the bushes and swept across the faces of the three spectators of fate. Yanchi lit another tailor made cigarette, drew upon it, and then passed it to his brother, who in turn drew long and hard and then passed it on to Smiljana. The words that hung in the air now seemed to echo inside their heads. "No way out. No way out."

Radovan looked as nervous as he felt. He walked on the quiet and lonely road looking out over the fields. The small plots of land owned by different farmers reflected the various usages of different fertilizers. Some of the corn pushed upward to the sky with pride whilst other fields seemed to be tired not even trying to defy gravity.

His mind was racing with all kinds of conflicting thoughts. He hated his brother he accepted this. He loved Irena he also accepted this. That he may be the father of Irena's child caused him great confusion. Suddenly and without any notice an elderly man was standing beside him. He must have just come out from the small green dirt pathway that led off into the fields.

The old man had gray almost white hair. He looked distinguished and for some reason important. "You look troubled." He spoke with authority and also with a compassionate edge to his voice. Radovan was suspicious and at first did not respond.

The old man smiled and spoke again. "You look like you are about to make a big decision." Radovan now felt both nervous and afraid yet somehow the presence that the man carried with him caused him to allow his guard to come down.

He spoke almost marveling at his freedom to share with

the stranger. "I am troubled and I have to make a decision." The old man smiled and then put his hand on his younger companion's shoulder and started to walk.

Radovan felt as if resistance was impossible to such goodness and found himself walking and listening as a student listens to the first words of a teacher who embodies both wisdom and grace. The old man, still with his arm on his shoulder as they walked smiled and then spoke, "Does your decision involve someone else?" Before he could answer the mystery man spoke again. "You have to ask yourself only one question, and that is 'What must I do to be right rather than feel right?' Feeling right makes your decision selfish, doing right to be right will always make your decision unselfish."

For one moment Radovan felt as if everything around him was suddenly silent. He stopped and closed his eyes and thought to himself, "Doing right not feeling right." The very thought was frightening and yet made him feel noble and strong. He opened his eyes to speak again with his newfound teacher only to discover himself alone on the country road. A gentle warm breeze rushed by him and he felt both afraid and full of expectation. A white dove flew gently past him as the mystery of life took a strange turn in his pilgrimage.


Stefan looked across the room. Maria and Darko sat at the table holding hands and laughing. Stefan had been wearing his cross and chain again for some years but now it meant so much more to him than when he had taken it off all those years ago in the forest near his home. It was now time for him to make his own way in life. It was now time to go to high school and then to University and study Social Work. Darko, the ever-joyful never depressed social worker, was his model. He wanted his life, like Darko, to mean something. He wanted to love people in the way that Ivan and

Jasmina did. Most of all he felt this overwhelming urge to bring God into other people's lives just as God had been brought into his own life.

Irena sat in the chair alone. Her baby, Milena, nursed at her breast quietly, the warmth and the joy that Irena experienced was intense, as something of her life and essence passed through her body to this baby she loved so dearly.

She stroked the baby's hair that already had a slight copper tint to it. The little chip missing from her ear coupled to the hair confirmed what she thought was true. The baby was her own and Radovan's. She gently stroked the baby's unbearably soft face and then felt for the fragile hip of the little one that was now deformed.

The doctor had said that she would always walk with a limp. For Irena it was the curse. She had sinned with Radovan and now all of them were cursed and there was no way out. Suddenly the door opened and Radovan walked into the room. He looked at Irena. He loved her. He held out his hands and asked to hold the baby. He looked at the hair and the ear of the little one and asked, "It is, isn't it?" Irena whispered and nodded. Gently he passed the baby to Irena and turned and looked out of the window. "I'm going away." The words were like a knife that seemed to dig at her already broken heart. "But I will always love you and I will find some way of supporting this child." Irena began to cry. Radovan reached out his hand and gently touched her face. She rubbed her cheek against his hand and kissed it, her tears covering both his hand and her face. As the door closed she began to moan and hold the baby closer to herself. He paused at the door and looked back one last time. " There will never be anyone else, there never could be."

# The Roma Chronicles

Yanchi sat on the chair looking at his cousin. He was there but everything was blurred by the effect of drinking so much wine. His cousin reached his hand and passed another glass to him. "So now I am a father, I have a child but she is cursed and deformed. We are all cursed I should never have married that stupid woman. She is so stupid."

Yanchi's cousin looked across room. "She is stupid because she married you, no one else would." Yanchi burst out laughing. "I know! I know!"

He drank his fifteenth glass of wine and continued barely able to get the words out. "I know but I will make her pay for all of this." He laughed again. "Do you remember when we were little, when we would take those little puppies and slowly strangle them?"

His cousin threw a pornographic magazine over to him. "Read this, this will make you a man." Yanchi for a moment looked at the pictures of degradation and then spoke again laughing. "No listen to me, I'm going to do the same to my wife as I did to those puppies you see, I will, I will."

Radovan stood on the doorstep of the beautifully maintained house with lovely gardens. The early middle-aged Croat woman stood talking with him with a gentle compassionate smile. She held a leash in her hand with a faithful but young Labrador dog. There was a beauty in the woman's face despite her age. She nodded and touched Radovan on the shoulder. They shook hands and Radovan turned and walked away. The woman stood at the door watching him leave. He turned and smiled and they both raised a hand in farewell salute.

# 2
## Several Years Later

The sun shone brightly through the dirty window. The warmth of its glow poured down upon Milena as she lay on the floor. Her nose was bleeding and already a bruise was forming around her left eye. She tried to raise herself up on her remaining arm that was not racked with pain. Her hip, being deformed, made her look almost like a reptile as she tried to drag herself up to the point where she could reach the chair to assist herself in upward motion. Her teenage eyes were aged beyond theiSr natural process. They had a frightened look. They were dark brown, deep and warm, filled with a depth that comes only through suffering.

Standing above her was her father, Yanchi. He had a large stomach that pushed past the shirt and the undershirt whose task it was to reign it in. His face was covered with dark stubble that appeared to be a permanent feature upon his face. He looked down upon his daughter trying to raise herself up. He loathed her. Her shiny hair with a blue-black tint covered her face as she tried in desperation to get up.

With a vicious kick his foot snapped upon her arm that she was trying in vain to raise herself with. Her face smashed to the concrete with a sound and the effect of a hard-boiled egg being stepped on. She cried. Without saying a word. Yanchi walked out of his house. Milena lay on the floor weeping with pain and bitter sadness. The door opened and her mother screamed as she rushed in.

Irena was a thin worn out young woman, her face had deep lines and her hands were large. She wore a cheap long skirt that came down to her ankles and a thin T-shirt. She turned to her daughter and then to the door that opened up onto the village. She screamed and threw her hands into a forward action several times pronouncing a curse upon her husband. Then with equal tenderness to what had been anger she gently gathered her daughter up from the floor and laid her on the bed that was pushed against the wall.

The young woman's face appeared to be the meeting place of disappointment and confusion. "Why does he hate me so much? What have I done to make him hate me in this way?" Irena held her child close. "It will be O.K. one day, you will see, we will move away, and he will never find us. It will be you and me together, no one else, you'll see."

Milena had heard the words so many times before and even now they still bought some kind of hope. "Mama, Teta Nada gave me a new book, I don't know why she keeps giving me these books, but this one is different, it is a holy book."

Milena, despite the pain, reached behind the bed and pulled out a box of books. Teta Nada had been giving books to Milena for some years. She had started by sharing children's books and had gradually started introducing novels. Irena held the Holy Book in her hands. She felt nervous, being such a sinner, holding such holy things.

Suddenly, she jumped up and poured a glass of water speaking rapidly as she worked. "I heard of this somewhere that if you dip a page of a holy book in a glass of water and drink it, it will lift any curse that you have on you, quick, drink it."

She held the glass out to her daughter who sat without moving. Her eyes were closed. A tear worked itself loose and tumbled down her cheek. "Oh Mama, I don't believe these things, if there is a curse, drinking this won't send it away."

Irena stopped and sat down. She wanted to share with her daughter that the curse that had caused her deformity in her hip and

## Jasmina, Darko and Milena

had brought the hatred of Yanchi upon her was because she, Irena, had sinned by loving and laying with Radovan. How she longed to tell her everything and allow them both to be joined in their secrets. Most of all she wanted someone to tell her how she could be set free from the great weight of guilt that she felt day and night.

An envelope was sitting on the table. The table was a beautiful dark and valuable wood, the legs were crafted by hand which one almost knew instinctively that they were hand crafted rather than turned out by a machine. The living room in Darko, Maria, and Stefan's apartment was a reflection of all their lives. The beautiful table came from Maria's family and had been handed down in the family for generations. As if by a ritual each time it found itself in a new home it would be taken and professionally restored.

On the walls, were the glass paintings of Naive Art. There was a Generalic nestled among the lesser-known painters, which like the table had been a gift in the family. There was a piece of wood that had been cut from the roof of an old house. It had come from the tiny one room dwelling that Darko had grown up in before he had been given out as a foster child. Stefan's piano was new. He had worked so hard to save up to buy the instrument. In the evenings he would play deep from within himself as if the agony of loss by war flowed through his playing.

As he played Marija would cry. The memories of her own loss, the gift of Stefan as an adopted son and the love a good man in Darko, all flowed together causing sadness and joy to be separated by a very thin membrane of emotion.

Maria spoke as Stefan walked into the room. "There is an official-looking letter for you on the table." Stefan tore open the envelope as he leaned back in the chair. Maria could see by his face that something was wrong. He handed the letter to her who read and then spoke. "It looks to me that you have suddenly become rich."

Yanchi leaned back on his chair and drank another glass of cheap wine, Nina, a prostitute, drank from another glass. She had that unusual ability to out-drink her customers yet show no signs of being drunk. She spoke as she lit a cigarette. "You've been coming here for years and I don't think you've washed once in that whole time." Yanchi laughed. "It's my way, it's my way."

Milena held a candle in one hand and the Holy Book in the other. Her mother was asleep in the darkness. She had no idea where her father was. She loved this time of the night. On weekdays it was so quiet. Sometimes there would be the odd man coming home drunk or the shout of another to his wife to keep the baby quiet. Generally, though, this was a time of peace. This was her time. She would read long into the night from the books Teta Nada had given her. Here she was free in her imagination.   Sometimes she would find herself so connecting to the characters that she would act out scenes in her mind with herself in the story. There would be a young man who would take her on rides in a horse and carriage. They would talk to each other and he would call her 'Miss Milena'. Then he would say something like, "Miss Milena, I am interested in what you have to say about life." At other times he would bow in a crowded ballroom and take her hand to dance. Oh how she could dance. She could walk and run and there was no talk of curses and no hateful words. She would then see herself holding a little baby close to her breast. Her husband, who was strong yet gentle, would be standing there to protect them both from anyone who would hurt them.

## *Jasmina, Darko and Milena*

Tonight was different, very different. Teta Nada had given her the Holy Book but had placed a marker inside and underlined a story for her to read. She read it holding the candle and found herself shaking, she read it again and again, each time the shaking sensation increased. She placed the book back in the box and then in one gentle puff sent the light of the candle to the place of memories. She lay down on the bed next to her mother, dogs would occasionally bark but the silence seemed to surround her. She found herself shaking again. She then prayed for the first time in her life. "Oh God, can this be true what I have just read, can this really be true?"

# 3
## Daddy God

Stefan walked into the office for the interview with a sense of confidence but also with clear understanding that he may not even be considered for the job. Being a Serb was not easy in Croatia and the day the police came to the flat to question Maria about his ethnic identity still stayed in his mind. Growing up in the school system had been hard but rather then break him it seemed to push him on to excel in his studies.

The office was dark and dreary, on the wall was a calendar celebrating Croatia's national football team, there was a large caption with the word "Glory." Underneath someone had cynically written the latest unemployment figures.

There were three female secretaries sitting at desks that gave the appearance of tiredness and decay with papers piled up as if waiting for a day that would never come. Each of the women had blank unsmiling faces. The youngest, in her twenties, had hair a color that gave the impression that it was supposed to be one way when in fact had turned out to be the very opposite.

The other two women looked at fashion magazines not acknowledging that he had come into the room. A door opened and a big man reached out his hand in a gracious manner and welcomed Stefan into his office. "So you are Darko's boy. Your dad and I go back all the way to kindergarten together, funny thing is I never knew he had Gypsy blood so it was as much a surprise to me as it was to everyone else."

Stefan smiled and nodded. He was relieved that the principle of who-you-know not what-you-know was just kicking into high

## Jasmina, Darko and Milena

gear. "I spoke with Darko yesterday and I told him I would do what I could." Stefan smiled again. "Thank you Sir, I have brought my papers with me and my university credentials." The big man interrupted. "I don't need to see those, Darko's word is good enough and I have already decided what to do with you."

He stood up and walked across the room and opened a window and lit a cigarette as he continued to speak. "The E.U. has given us money for minority development projects, you are a minority and I am surrounded up here in Medjimurije by minorities."

Stefan felt nervous as he always did when the word minority was used. "Anyway, I can give you a job for three years funded by the E.U.." He laughed as he sat down again. "The joke is they have so much money and so much guilt. Guilt and money is very good business for us. Well, enough, I have to get back and change the world, so you start the first of next month, which is, let me see, the Monday after next. Tell Darko he owes me on this one."

The big man stood up smiling and reached out to shake Stefan's hand. "Sorry for interrupting, Sir, but what is the job?"

The big man laughed out loud. "Anything you want it to be but it has to involve Gypsies, just write up some ideas, anything you like, it just has to have Gypsies all over the place."

Stefan by now was standing and shaking hands. "Thank you, Sir, I would like to think it through how to best serve the needs of the Roma community."

The big man laughed. "Of course we have to call them Roma now, especially now that old Darko is blessed with that special blood. Make sure you use that word in the proposal. 'Roma Cultural Development' anything like that, the E.U. loves all that kind of stuff."

The big man paused for a moment and then spoke again. "Hey, listen to this one, what do you see at the top of a Gypsy ladder?" He paused while Stefan looked on embarrassed. "A sign that says stop." The big man laughed loudly as he guided Stefan past the secretaries to the main door. They shook hands again and Stefan was left standing in the street not sure if he was happy or sad.

Yanchi sat on a chair next to a table in a dingy and dark corner of an equally dingy and dark bar. Sitting opposite him was his soul mate of the bottle, Tomislav.

Tomislav was about sixty years old, to look at him, he could have been eighty years old as he had made the abuse of alcohol an art-form for a very long time. He was as was customary for a man of his vocation unshaven. He had yellow teeth that were just on the edge of turning green. His almost bald head was oily and his eyes were milky and perpetually leaking. A smell not unlike rotten eggs seemed to follow him as a companion.

He spoke. "I want a woman." Yanchi laughed. "Then have a woman." Tomislav drunk from a glass of strong but cheap spirits that would have been better employed cleaning the inside of a watch made about the time that he had been born.

"No, I want a woman in my house to be a slave, you know a real slave, I'm getting old and starting to mess myself in the night." Yanchi laughed. He liked Tomislav he was man after his own heart. "Well get some old worn-out Baka who's lost her old man and whose kids don't want her living with them."

Tomislav drank again and looked up. "Actually I was thinking about a gypsy girl, you know a young gypsy girl that can be my slave. I hear you can buy them."

Yanchi felt a twinge of offence then brushed it off. "You can buy one, but it would cost too much for you, as you are a dirty old scum bag like me." "How much is too much?" Yanchi laughed, drank, and leaned forward. "Too much for you."

## Jasmina, Darko and Milena

Milena sat alone with the candle and the Holy Book. Her mother was asleep after drinking herself into tearful unconsciousness. Milena read the same passage that she had read before and as before she found herself shaking. She had begun quite a conversation with her new unseen friend and had started to call him 'daddy'. At first it was strange but she had read one of the places that Teta Nada had underlined that said we are to call God 'daddy'. As the nights of reading had gone on, she always started by saying a prayer. "Daddy God, show me something lovely tonight in my Holy Book."

It seemed He always did and the dirty run down two-room house became a sacred place night after night. She looked over at her mother laying asleep fully clothed. Her hand hung over the bed with her finger tips just a whisper away from an empty beer bottle that was laying discarded after fulfilling its duty. Milena loved her mother. She reminded her of some of the sad characters in her books. "Daddy God, could you bring my Mama some peace in her life?"

Teta Nada held the telephone and listened, she listened and then spoke with kindness. "Milena seems to be doing well. I give them the meat and the vegetables every week from the money you send and I give Milena books all the time, she is becoming quite the reader."

Radovan found himself becoming emotional and his voice began to shake as he spoke of both Milena and Irena.

Teta Nada spoke again. "As I have said to you before, it is important that Milena knows that you are her father. Irena also needs to tell her husband as these secrets only end up hurting everyone."

Radovan spoke of how different it was in their culture. He then thanked her for all the care and love she had shown to them. Teta Nada hung up the telephone. She was an elderly woman who did not show her age. There was a refinement and a beauty about her. She prayed. "Lord Jesus, you know these people better then they know themselves, bring peace and goodness into this place."

# 4

## The Book

Stefan and Darko walked to their car after leaving the lawyers office. It was cloudy with a dampness to the air but no real chill to speak of. Winter was though beginning to threaten its' presence. Inside the car Darko took the folder, read it through, and then spoke in a quiet but fatherly manner. "Okay, everything is in order, your parent's home in Serbia has been sold to the U.N. Rehousing Program. You have been given this piece of land in the Podravina, which is valued at 60,000 Euros. You can sell it, keep it or do what you want with it."

Stefan took the folder without saying a word. He nodded without turning his head. His mind was full of the memories from all those years ago when his parents were murdered by their own people. Darko put his arm around his shoulder. "I love you man, you have come a long, long way. " Stefan nodded again. For a moment the car seemed to be filled with a deep peace that flowed from Darko to his stepson.

For Milena to ride a bike was possible but not without great effort. She stood holding the bike and then managed to lean it against the wall and climb on using her left foot to help her balance. She then swiveled her deformed hip and right leg into place pulling away from the wall and then with one hand on the handlebar and one hand on the wall she would then push herself off. Once she was going she was fine.

She, like many of the women in the village, went on their

bikes into town. Some would scavenge through rubbish whereas some, like Milena, would have a kind local lady they would visit to be given food. Very often the food was leftover but in Milena's case Teta Nada would give every week some good meat and vegetables.

The roads were becoming more and more slippery as winter came. She could almost hear the echo of her father's voice saying he wished a truck would run her over and kill her.

Arriving at her destination and getting off her bike was similar to the start of her journey but in reverse. She clumsily dismounted and then hobbled up to the gate of Teta Nada's house and rang the bell. There was an instant response of a dog barking and then the voice of Teta Nada saying, "Be quiet, Bela, be quiet."

There was a fire glowing in the living room and as Milena sat down on a warm and comfortable chair drinking hot fruit tea she imagined that she was in the scene from one of her books. Teta Nada sat opposite and both looked into the flames that danced with irregular joy around the burning wood.

"Teta Nada, forgive me for asking such a personal question, but why have you shown so much kindness to me over all these years." Teta Nada smiled but continued to look into the fire. Then spoke with warmth in her voice that equaled the atmosphere of the log fire. "I gave you a Bible just recently and in the Bible it says that the greatest thing in life is to love God with all our heart and to love other people as much as we care about ourselves."

There was a childlike charm in Milena's voice as she spoke. "I have read the Bible you gave me, and there is one part that you marked for me to read that every time I read it I shake all over. It is like I get this excitement in my stomach that then rushes all over my body."

She shivered as the memory of the experience was relived as she sat and talked with this older wiser woman. She then continued. "And every night now I pray and when I pray I say Daddy God help my mother to be happy and help me to be good."

Teta Nada smiled with a tear forming in her left eye. "You are very precious Milena, and I think God has something wonderful for you in your life."

Milena looked serious. "It is hard to believe that anything good could happen to me, but you are good, the books are good, and the Bible is very good."

Teta Nada reached out her hand, "I mean something much greater then these things. I pray for you every day so let's wait and see what God has for you." Milena smiled and then what seemed to be a cloud of sadness came over her. "You know I want to be good and I want God to love me but I don't think He can, it is like I'm unlovable because of the curse." Teta Nada did not speak but gently placed her hand on Milena's arm.

Stefan walked into his new office. The big man was there waiting for him. The three ladies greeted him this time with a certain warmth and acceptance. He was shown his desk, which was opposite the young woman with hair in need of healing. The big man introduced Stefan to the ladies and then spoke. "Okay let's get the important things over first, here is the swear box. Every time someone swears they have to put some money in the swear box. The rest of the people in the office assess how bad the language is and then calculate how much money has to go in the box."

Stefan laughed. "Who gets the money?" The big man picked up the box and clutched it close to his chest. "We give 10% to the church to buy Catholic seals, as you can see, by the seals on the window this is a profane place, the other 90% pays for pizza once a week for everyone in the office."

He paused then looked serious. "For the sake of the Mother

# The Roma Chronicles

Church and our stomach's I command you Stefan the Minority to swear, swear, swear."

After the initiation he sat opposite the big man who was reading his proposal. He nodded and made positive raises of his eyebrows and grunted semi-human sounds of approval. "Okay, I think I have it, I also think I see some Darko in here, may he live long and not have many more children to torment us all."

Stefan smiled. "He did help me develop the ideas, Sir." "I can see that, but this is good. So you will take a Gypsy, sorry, a Roma village and survey the number of adults who can read the form for the renewal of a lost I.D. card and then come up with some incentive to get them helping each other into filling out forms." "Yes, Sir, exactly, I have gone through the Social Services list of villages and I think I want to go to this one."

He pointed to a name on a list. "You are a lamb ready to become someone's dinner, but why not, have a go, the E.U. is paying for it."

Stefan felt affirmed despite the almost careless manner of the big man. "By the way do you know how you can recognize a Gypsy house? They have locks on their trash cans." He burst out laughing at his own joke and passed the folder back to Stefan. "Okay, get to work, let's change the world."

Irena sat on the floor. She held a bottle of cheap wine in her hands, which hung limply in her lap. There was a beauty about her in the same way there was about Milena. Her beauty though was rapidly fading and it was nights like this night that were the source of her downward journey.

She was drunk to the last stage just before passing out. She spoke to an imaginary audience seated in the room. It was as if she were the prosecutor and the ghosts were the jury. The drink slurred her speech.

"I am not a bad person all the time, but I am a bad person, you know that if I had married Radovan instead of this dog, may the meat rot on his bones, I would have been someone special, I probably would have a three or four bedroom house with a toilet and even a bathtub, but this dog has made us live like pigs."
She shouted another string of curses at her absent husband. "But you know I am guilty, I am guilty, guilty, guilty! I hate myself! Oh Radovan! Radovan! Radovan!" She drank some more then transferred the agony of her conscious world for the torment of her dreams.

# 5
## The Meeting

Stefan knocked on the door. The condition of the village was worse than he had imagined. The sense of resignation to despair seemed to cling to his heart like the smell of fat on one's clothes when standing close to a grill.

From the house came a muddled command to enter. Sitting on a chair and leaning against a table and reading a book was Milena. Her hair was black but not just in monotone, it seemed to be alive with variance and a gradation color. Her warm, innocent deep brown eyes seemed to dance as if she had never witnessed evil and yet they were eyes that were deep that came only from suffering. Her skin was olive rather than dark with almost fresh peach-like cheeks. Her teeth were white and unusually straight. Her neck had a sensual beauty to it that only magnified what Stefan perceived as being beauty.

Without realizing his star-struck manner he spoke. "You are reading a book?"

Milena looked down at the book and then up at the face of the intruder. He may have intruded but his eyes, his manner, and even the way he stood gave her a sense that this was someone she could trust. She spoke in reply. "Yes, it is, it is the Bible." Stefan gasped. "The Bible, are you a Christian?"

Milena looked confused. Immediately Stefan redeemed himself. "I apologize I should not have burst in like this, I am from Social and I am doing a survey on adults who can read, my name is

Stefan." He reached out his hand and very gently shook hers. "Its okay, my name is Milena Orshus."

"Well, Miss Milena, I apologize again for intruding but I would be very interested to hear your ideas about reading, especially the Bible, as I read the Bible every day."

It was now Milena's turn to gasp. For one moment she thought she would pass out. This handsome young man had called her 'Miss Milena' and he was interested in her ideas. Her eyes were glassy. She spoke in a giddy intoxicated way. "Do you have a horse and carriage outside?"

Stefan looked puzzled, "No, I came by car." Now it was Milena's turn to apologize. "I'm sorry, you caught me off balance." Stefan smiled.
"No problem, but may I sit down and talk about your reading skills?"

Stefan sat with his notepad open and went through a list of questions. He was stunned by the whole experience. He realized as he had talked, that in looks and mannerisms Milena reminded him of his dead mother. The smile, the head leaning to one side when answering a question, the use of her hands to make a point. For a moment he paused looking down at his pad and he thought to himself. "This is the most beautiful girl I have ever seen in my life. "

He spoke again. "Forgive me for all of these questions but tell me about the Bible how is it that you are reading it?"

Milena went on to explain about Teta Nada and how she prayed to Daddy God. She then found herself free to trust him with the passage of the Bible that had caused her to shake all over. She turned to the page and read it to him. Stefan smiled, and looked directly into her eyes.

"Well, it is the story of a woman whose body was deformed and had been for eighteen years and then Jesus healed her." Milena seemed to shiver. "Yes, but do you think God still heals people like that today?" Stefan paused, "I do, why not, sure, He can do that today if He wants to."

They continued to talk and then Stefan excused himself, as he had to be back at the office. Milena stood up and then in labored and contorted fashion limped to the door. Stefan felt a rush of sweat run up his back onto his neck and at the same time a wave of nausea swept over him. He tried to suppress it but his face turned a shocking red as his mouth became dry.

Milena spoke. "Thank you for coming, you have really helped me." Stefan shook her hand. "Miss Milena, thank you for the time." He stammered. "Can I visit you again?" "Of course I want to talk with you some more."

Stefan drove away from the village with his mind swimming. He could not believe that such an experience could happen. He played back the whole scene again and again. Regretting that he had been so definite about the healing he could have kicked himself. But this woman was utterly beautiful, gentle, precious and openhearted to God. He prayed and then realized he was shouting at God. "Lord, what are you doing to me?"


Radovan hung up the telephone from speaking to Teta Nada. He thought to himself that she was such a good woman. Some of the Christians he had met had been awful yet Teta Nada was filled with a sense of goodness that made him think about God. It was the same feeling he had experienced after meeting that man on the country road who had told him to do what was right not what made him feel good. That experience had stayed with him and had started some kind of response inside of him.

He knew he was going to love Irena for the rest of his life and he knew he was going to love his daughter whom he had never seen. He had gone to the Catholic Church and had lit a candle for them both and said some Hail Mary prayers for them. The experience had created a strange conflict within him. He felt connected to them by lighting the candle but something inside of him had this strange feeling he was not supposed to do the Hail Mary for them. He was very confused. What he did know was that something was stirring within him and he sensed that God was near him. He could not explain it, neither did he feel as if he even wanted to explain it but God was near.

Milena was riding her bike on the main road just outside of the village. Her mind had been so full of thoughts of God and the Bible especially after the visit from Stefan. Suddenly she noticed a slow walking tortoise trying to cross the road. She could see a car coming toward them. A rush of panic ran through her as she realized the tortoise was going to be squashed.

She dropped her bike to the ground and as quickly as she could she limped towards the tortoise. The car was not going to slow down. She raised her hand to stop the car while standing in the middle of the road. The driver angrily blasted the car horn for her to move but she continued to limp toward the tortoise. The car was forced to stop just as she picked up the tortoise that had now retreated to the safety of its shell. The driver leaned out of the window and shouted at Milena.

She smiled and limped toward the car. The man was angry and his face was red with pulsating rage. "Are you crazy, you stupid Gypsy cow, you could have got killed!" Milena looked at the man in the face.

"I am sorry that it disturbed you but do not speak like that to me."

The man was going to let loose another tirade but something

stronger in her than what was in himself was in a strange and mysterious way detected. He looked at her in stunned silence. Milena smiled and then spoke, "Anyway this little one can go on living a little longer, thank you for stopping." The man felt an immediate sense of guilt the quietly nodded. He rolled up his window and slowly drove away.

Yanchi sat alone in the house. He thought back over the years of his life. He was not a bad person he thought to himself. He was always misunderstood. He thought of his wife Irena. He had never loved her. He had often wondered why he stayed with her. In fact he could not stand her and he hated Milena even more. It was not right that he should have been cursed with these two women who were so ugly to him. Every time Milena walked in front of him it made him feel sick. She was the reason why everything had gone wrong in his life. He poured himself another glass of cheap wine.

He was a good person really but stuck with two bad women. Maybe in some strange way he would eventually be blessed and they would both die. A chill rain through his heart at the thought. Who would look after him, do the cooking and cleaning. He felt frustrated that he was stuck in a corner and could not get out.

# 6

## With Cream Please

The small open-air café in the center of town had for generations been the meeting place of lovers, revolutionaries and radicals. There were about 10 tables scattered around underneath a large umbrella like awning. The summer had ended and so had the crowds but it was still warm enough to sit outside which was also a relief from the thick cigarette smoke that hung as a constant vapor inside.

Stefan sat at a table drinking alone. He drank latté as he had always had since he was a young man whenever he was out. At home he was a four shot a day espresso person.

He could feel a certain sense of anxiety and excitement about meeting Milena here. This was his world and they had only ever spent time in her village. As she rode up on her bicycle his heart leapt within himself. She got off her bike and awkwardly made her way over to where he was. He stood up to greet her and was not sure if he should kiss her on each cheek or shake hands. The dilemma was settled as with smiling face she reached out her hand to shake his.

For obvious reasons they were both nervous. Faster than usual a young woman holding a round pewter tray came and asked what they would like to drink. Both of them sensed the contempt in the non-verbal atmosphere that surrounded the young waitress. Stefan passed a menu over to Milena and then asked her what she wanted. Milena, at ease with herself, looked at the menu and then smiled at the waitress in a disarming way. "You know I have never been in a café before, I do not know how to act or what to ask for."

The young contemptuous waitress was visibly moved. She sat down between the two and carefully went through the list of coffees and hot and cold drinks. Milena smiled and thanked the young woman and ordered a hot chocolate with cream.

Stefan looked on in a way that only a man who has had his heart melted would do so. He smiled and then spoke. "You are very relaxed and self-confident for someone who does not visit these places much." She blushed and looked down. "Well, I am me, a broken body, a gypsy, a poor person but I was reading in the New Testament this week about Jesus telling his followers about a man who had a big party and invited those kinds of people along."

Stefan smiled and wondered what it must be like to be a complete blank slate without any history of religion in ones heart, suddenly discovering Jesus in the pages of the New Testament. "Also, for days now I have been thinking and praying about my sin and how Jesus wants to release me from it."

She explained how she realized that even though people thought of her as a good person she knew that she was actually not if she used God as the standard to compare herself to.

Stefan felt overwhelmed and then spoke. "It seems to me that God is showing you the way without anyone to guide you. That is very special." She smiled and carried on. "Well, I think you are right but I do have so many questions, especially about if I can be healed like the woman we talked about in the Bible."

Before Stefan could answer the waitress brought the drinks back. He excused himself as a phone call came through on his cell phone. He stood up, motioned his apologies and walked a few feet away to talk. The waitress served the drinks and was just about to leave, stopped and turned and looked at Milena. "You are different from any gypsy I have ever met before."

Milena smiled, blushed and gently shrugged her shoulders.

"Thank you and forgive me for saying this but you are a lovely looking person and you do not need to wear these kinds of clothes that show so much of your body to be attractive, you are lovely in yourself."

The waitress stood stunned. No one had ever spoken to her in this way before in her life. Who was this girl she wondered to herself. Stefan returned and apologized and sat down not realizing what had happened.

Milena drank from the hot chocolate and quietly giggled. "Look at this cream Stefan I have never had anything like this, anyway tell me about healing."

Stefan looked down not knowing quite how to respond. "Okay, let me tell you the truth, I don't know how healing works, it's only when I saw you after you stood up at the house that day that I realized how this subject may affect you."

Milena sat silent then spoke. "You know I really have no expectations, even this chocolate is something completely new with cream on top. I think if God wants to heal me He will and I was wondering why after reading that story why I would shake so much all over."

Stefan realized that each minute that he was with this girl in her innocence he was being drawn into a deep vortex of love. The waitress came back and said that she was leaving and could they pay the bill. She gave Stefan some change and then looked at Milena. "Can you come back again and visit me so we can talk, my name is Lydia." Milena smiled and nodded. Stefan wondered what had transpired.

Jasmina was like a sister to Stefan. He had always thought of her as so much older than himself even though they were just a few years apart. Stefan sat in the kitchen as Jasmina busied herself. " Do you want some Sirinica?" Stefan laughed, " Yes, but don't let the Croats hear you call it that or they will report you to the culture police." Jasmina looked in a disproving way. " Ivan calls it Sirinica all the time and you and I both are very blessed to live here." Stefan raised his hand. " I know I am sorry, I did not mean to hurt you."

Jasmina smiled, kissed him on his forehead and put a plate of the cheese pastry in front of him. Stefan looked on at Jasmina working and then spoke.

" Jas, I am in love with a Roma girl, she is Bayash like my Dad, not Arli like you." Jasmina sat down and looked closely and then deeply into Stefan's eyes.

He continued. " She is very spiritual and loves Jesus. Actually, she is wonderful." Jasmina smiled and spoke. " And what does her family say and what do Darko and Maria say?"

He played with the pastry with his fork. " Well, the truth is you are only one that knows that I am in love with her, you see, well, she does not know yet either."

Milena had awkwardly stopped her bike on the bridge crossing the Drava River. In what was to her normal, but to an onlooker clumsy, she got off her bike and rested it against the side of the bridge. She looked downstream towards the east.

She remembered the stories that she had heard of her ancestors traveling along the river. They had been slaves in Romania for nearly 400 years and had been treated like livestock. She wondered why it was that people could be so cruel. Her own father was so wicked and so cruel to both her mother and herself.

She wondered if they had all inherited evil from each another. As she was thinking a cold uneasy feeling came over her. It was as if all of a sudden she had become aware of something about herself that was so deep she could not put it into words.

She thought for a moment and bit her lip as she pondered. Evil behavior was something that she had lived with all her life. Her father was the most evil of men and compared to him her mother was not evil yet to be honest if she compared her mother to herself then it would be her mother that would seem evil but she Milena would appear good. Yet compare herself to Teta Nada and she Milena would appear to be evil and compare Teta Nada to Stefan and, the thoughts continued to race around in her mind.

She would not use these words but she was sensing evil was not an issue of behavior it was an issue of essence. As she stood looking down the river a sense of the light suddenly coming into her mind flooded through her. "Oh Daddy God, I understand, you are the one we have to compare ourselves to, not each other, we are all the same to you because you are so pure."

The awareness that she had stumbled upon the most supreme truth gave her a sense of destiny and yet still with the question ringing in her mind that if everyone was evil in God's sight what must be done? She experienced something very deep in these moments looking at the strong current-driven river force it's way through the crowd of nature towards its yet unknown destination.

# 7
## Suicide

Stefan and Milena sat again in what was now becoming "their" café. Lydia served them their usual drinks. Milena spoke looking more serious than usual.

"Can you help me with something?" Stefan nodded and she continued. "I think I am very close to understanding things more clearly, it seems that every day God shows me something new but, but why did Jesus really have to die?"

Stefan drank his coffee and pondered on the question. Milena sat in her usual chair. Her hair was pulled back under a scarf. She looked so small and childlike yet she was so mature and open.

"You know where it talks about the law of God being his standard or his desire for us to live, well the Bible says that everyone breaks the law."

Milena nodded. "I know, I think that was what I was realizing down by the river."

Stefan continued. "Well, the Bible says that sin has to be punished." Milena nodded again in agreement. "I get that as well but I was wondering why doesn't God just forgive everyone?" "Good question but would God be good if he allowed evil to go unpunished?"

She smiled. "I understand, it is because He is good that He cannot allow sin to go unpunished." Stefan stood up stretched and then sat down again. He pondered for a moment took a sip of coffee and then spoke again.

"Jesus lived on earth and did not break the law and because he was perfect he was the only one who could take your punishment in your place. It is hard to get this but God put your punishment on Jesus when Jesus died on the cross. Because he was the only one who was perfect he was the only one who could take our place."

She nodded in a knowing way is if a suspicion had suddenly been confirmed. "That is why the Bible talks about the substitute where He died and He gave everything to take away my sins, right?"

Stefan nodded. Despite the fact they were in public Milena allowed the emotion of the moment to fill both her eyes and her words. She looked upward with tears streaming down her face. " I believe this now and I am ready for anything that you may have for me to do."

Teta Nada was standing at the sink washing some dishes when she had a sudden and strange feeling inside that something was wrong in the Roma village. She looked out of the window almost expecting to see Milena ride up.

She walked into the living room and stroked Bela before sitting down. Suddenly, she was gripped with a need to pray and found herself calling out to God to protect Milena and Irena and Radovan. The time passed and she found herself weeping in deep spiritual pain for each of them. Then without any understandable reason she felt a great wave of peace waft over her heart and found herself thanking and praising God for His hand on all their lives.

Irena was drunk again. This time was different. She had often used the contents of bottles like this one to numb, usually successfully, the sense of dark guilt that she felt almost every day. The drink mocked her, as day after day she would need more to sustain the relief from the psychic sorrow that she experienced like a patient with a terminal illness.

This morning she was drinking to help prepare her for death. The sheer weight and burden of living had become so much greater than any fear of dying that she may have had. She was going to Hell so why not now as later. Teta Nada would care for Milena and her death would also prove to her husband that he no longer controlled her life.

She had walked up to the shop near the village. The girl behind the cash registrar looked surprised that she had spent so much on a large bottle of Gordan's Gin. Usually, she would buy cheap wine and perhaps on the second Tuesday of the month she would buy beer. She placed the half empty bottle on the table and carefully washed and dried a glass and placed it next to it.

She had drunk the first half straight from the bottle to numb her mind but now she was going to celebrate by slowly drinking the rest.

She had one nice outfit, which consisted of a white blouse and a lovely green nylon skirt. She had laid them out on the bed and occasionally she would straighten them out in preparation for what was to come.

She had worked hard on washing her hair and getting it exactly as she could remember it was when she first met Radovan. She had a few scraps of make-up that she had found in a bag of rubbish. As she applied it to her face using the mirror she found herself stunned at her own beauty.

She fought back the tears, as to smudge the make-up would not help her in the preparations. She remembered when she was a little girl and thought that life was beautiful. Maybe it could be beautiful but not for her. She then slipped on her fresh white blouse. Just the feel of it on her skin gave her a sense of being in a special occasion.

## Jasmina, Darko and Milena

For a moment she considered shaving under her arms but decided against it. No one would be able to see anyway as the blouse had long sleeves. The skirt came next and immediately transformed her into something fresh and beautiful.

She took the small mirror and inspected herself all over moving the mirror up and down her body. She sat down at the table and poured another glass of gin and then began reciting, "Hail Mary full of grace..." The gin began to reinforce its earlier roll and she felt a warm glow passing all through her body. Then instinctively she knew it was now time and so rose and walked across the room. She stopped and turned and looked at the glass and saw a smudge of make-up. She wiped it clean using the small tablecloth that she had placed it on for the occasion.

The knife was long and thin and sharp. It was the kind used for cutting difficult pieces of meat from the bone. She sat on the edge of the bed and began to breathe deeply. She began to recite the Lord's Prayer but could only remember the first few lines. She thought of Radovan and Milena. She lay the knife down and sat quietly for a moment.

Stefan parked his car on the edge of the village and walked through the row of houses to Milena's home. The children had become used to him now and generally ignored him as he walked. Winter had arrived but the air seemed fresh and the sun as a late fugitive from the summer still produced that special feeling that it was good to be alive.

He had to visit the headman in the village and then quickly visit Irena. As he walked past Milena's house he thought of how God had worked so mysteriously to introduce them to each other.

Milena stayed to talk with Lydia. She was so moved by what was going on in her heart and yet she sensed that she should reach out to her new friend. Lydia sat down and looked at the espresso cup that she was turning round in a nervous circle.

She spoke quietly, "You shocked me the other day when you spoke in the way that you did. It actually made me frightened, like are you a witch or something like that?"

Milena did not smile but looked gently and compassionately into her eyes. "No, not a witch, just a young woman who has spent her whole life being treated like a thing not a person. I guess I saw the same signs in you, different in that you are revealing so much of your body to men to be accepted, but it is really the same."

Immediately Lydia's eyes filled with tears. "How could you know that just by looking at me?"

This time as she replied her face beamed with an innocent childlike smile. "Because I looked into your eyes and saw your soul, I saw the real you just for a moment, which is the person God wants you to be not the person that these men want you to be."

Lydia sat stunned and quiet. She wiped her eyes then whispered a response, "I have never heard anything like this in my life, what should I do?"

Milena laughed lovingly, "Well the way you are dressed today is a step in the right direction." Lydia blushed and then laughed. Milena continued, "Really, I am just beginning to understand things, my friend Stefan, is helping me understand the Bible."

Lydia nodded, "Is he your boyfriend?" The words were like a shock of cold water thrown upon her. She looked so red and then felt if she would faint. "No, not my boyfriend, but I do love him so much, no he is like a brother I always dreamed of, a father I never had, and a friend who never tries to hurt me."

Lydia smiled. "Then, if he is not your boyfriend does that mean I can have him?"
Milena laughed and pretended to flick cream from her spoon.

Irena took the knife and held it towards her stomach the blade so lethal gently touched her white blouse without cutting the fabric. She squeezed her eyes shut and then cried out Radovan's name and pushed the knife with all her strength into her stomach.

She gasped but felt nothing other than a strange sensation of both warmth and cold. She felt a sense of triumph yet tragedy all rolled into the same experience. She did not look down but with all the force that she could generate she tore the knife upwards with a wrenching action. For one moment she smiled and then fell backwards on the bed with her last conscious awareness being a knocking on the door.

Stefan knocked on the door but there was no answer. He called Irena's name. He was going to leave a message to say that Milena would be home soon. There was no answer and he was just going to leave when he felt this overwhelming urge to open the door, which he did.

Immediately he knew why. Irena was lying on her back with a long knife protruding from her stomach. Blood seemed to be everywhere. For a moment Stefan was back in his village with his parents lying dead on the blood soaked earth. As he looked at Irena and he felt as if he was back in Jasmina's house with her mother crucified and nailed to the door. He groaned in his spirit. In a strange way he had seen so much death and mutilation that he was able to intervene quickly, without hesitation, in this most dreadful of circumstances. It was as if the same power that clicked into action when he dragged Jasmina out of the village ignited within him now.

He immediately flicked his cell phone and called emergency services, he identified himself and was able to produce a rapid response that would not have been so forthcoming if it had been a Roma voice on the phone.

He checked Irena's pulse and was surprised that she was still alive. He took the last of the gin and poured it all over the wound. He gently laid Irena's head in his lap and began to pray in a forceful yet pleading manner.

He did not want anyone in the village to know what had happened at this stage or chaos would have ensued. It was only as the sound of the ambulance siren came closer and then into the village that the madness let loose. If Irena was not dead now, she would be very soon.


Tomislav poured another drink and passed it to Yanchi. There was a perpetual drip coming from his nose and his eyes. This, with the sour smell that clung to his body and the yellow and green coating to his teeth, gave him the appearance of something evil that belonged in a swamp rather than in a place of people.

Yanchi drank then took a cigarette from Tomislav's packet that was lying on the table. "I have already told you that it would cost maybe 2000 Euros to get a wife for you, you're just too old and too dirty." Tomislav reached into his pocket and took out his wallet, "I have 300 Euros, that's all I have, there has to be woman that I can buy for that."

Yanchi wanted to keep the conversation open as long as he could to extract more cigarettes and beer. "I will ask around but it is not enough even for a mentally handicapped one."

# 8
## The Painful Truth

Yanchi sat alone in his house. Milena had gone to the hospital, collected and taken there by Stefan in his car. He poured himself a drink and lit another cigarette from the one he had just finished smoking. The door flew open and Smiljana, Irena's sister stood in the doorway. Her raven black hair was tied back in a ponytail. Her low-cut T-shirt revealed a homemade tattoo of a bi-gone lover's name. Her eyes pierced with hatred and anger. She said nothing but just stared at Yanchi as he sat motionless. He spoke first. "She's like you, like all women, a selfish cow. Who will look after me now? That cursed deformed daughter of mine?" Smiljana wanted to scream but she knew she could do the most damage by keeping herself under control. "I am going back to the hospital, she is going to die, but before she dies I want you to know something. My sister never loved you, she despised you, she loved your brother Radovan."

Yanchi roared and threw the bottle that was in his hand. It smashed against the wall next to Smiljana who now could control herself no longer.

She screamed into the village. "Milena is not your daughter, she is Radovan's! She will never come back here again!"

Yanchi jumped up and staggered towards his sister-in-law intending to kill her if necessary. He faltered and then collapsed crashing to the floor. Smiljana stood above him. "You are filth, I hope this news torments you day and night." She slammed the door and was gone.

# The Roma Chronicles

Milena and Stefan sat alone and close to each other in the Hospital waiting room. After nearly four hours a nurse came to where they were sitting. She ushered them into the doctor's office, Milena struggled to stand up and walk which caused Stefan to love her even more and long to be her strength and help.

The doctor did not look up until they were both seated. He reached out his hand to Stefan to shake it but did not extend the same protocol to Milena. "You are the daughter I assume and you are the social worker?"

Stefan found himself flushed with anger at the doctor's attitude. "No, I'm Milena's friend I also happen to be a social worker. I found the mother when I was visiting the home."

The doctor raised his eyebrows in a dismissive manner. "Well, here is the news, she is probably going to be dead by morning." Milena thought she would faint. Stefan felt as if he wanted to hit the doctor.

He reached out his arm and enveloped Milena's weeping form. They both felt the ambiguity of the pain of the circumstances and the strange electric warmth that touch created within them.

Yanchi sat in his old car and started the engine. He often drove whilst drinking but tonight he was even more unsteady than normal. He decided to drive slowly as his determination to fulfill his mission was paramount in his thinking.

Tomislav was in his usual place sitting in the corner. Yanchi reached without asking and took a cigarette from the pack on the table. He slowly drew in and then released the smoke as he tilted

## Jasmina, Darko and Milena

his head back. "Okay, I have a woman for you. She's a teenager and she has a slight limp when she walks, but you can have her for 300 Euros."

Radovan stood next to his sister, Gordana, in the small viewing chapel in the graveyard. The room had the appearance of a miniature church but was about four meters square. There was a large crucifix on the wall just above the table on which the coffin was laid. The crucifix had been placed carefully after a practitioner had come to assess the cross point of the spiritual currents that ran through the graveyard. This cross point was chosen for the placing of the crucifix to get maximum advocacy and spiritual power applied to the body of the departed.

In this case the cold lifeless body that lay in the small casket was Vesna, not yet one year old. Radovan stood with his arm around his sister trying to comfort her in the loss of her only child.

Gordana held the baby's hand and groaned in her spirit. The father of the child had long since departed and other then Radovan who had been staying with her, she had no one to comfort her.

The baby had suddenly died the day before. There was no apparent reason and none had been looked for by the hospital. Her long straggly hair seemed even more tired and sad than usual.

She was tall and thin. Radovan was her full brother with the same mother and father. He would not talk about it but he was a good man and was caring for her since she had been deserted.

Vesna just a few days before had been a happy and healthy child but now was no more.

The graveyard attendant had come and gone and had now returned. He looked nervous as he approached Radovan who still held his sister in a comforting manner. He looked down at the open casket and the baby lying still and lifeless.

He spoke, "The priest sent me down with a message. Because the baby is not baptized he cannot come and do the funeral." Radovan's sister reached out to her baby scooping her dead body into her arms and began to wail. Radovan stood speechless, the graveyard attendant spoke again. "The priest said he could baptize the baby and backdate the certificate but you would have to pay 200 Euros. Or he said you if want you can just take the chance on your baby's soul and you can bury it yourself."

Radovan took the baby from his sister and placed her little body in the coffin. He then covered the little one with the burial cover and then put the lid on the casket. Without saying anything to the attendant he carried the coffin out to the graveyard. There were grand marble gravestones standing proudly as memorials to the loyal members of the One True Church.

Radovan walked through their giant marble statues to the small section at the far end of the graveyard where the gypsies were buried with just a small wooden stake as a marker.
He laid the casket down. He took the shovel that was awaiting the orders of the one who had requested his blood money and started digging a hole in the ground.

His sister knelt down and a laid on the tiny coffin. She repeated Vesna's name over and over again as she wept. Each shovel of dirt was thrown on the pile with an agonizing question forming in a prayer being uttered. "You are a good God, but these priests, why do you let them get away with it?" "I know you are there, here, everywhere but how can you let so much evil exist?" "I want to be a true believer but this is too much, can't you show me something good in all this?"

He gently placed the coffin into the ground and then shoveled the dirt into place. His sister was kneeling by the freshly displaced earth. Her hands soaked with her tears had earth upon them, which in turn found it's way onto her face and in her hair. She screamed with all the force that her tired voice could muster. "Mother of God, where is my baby?" Radovan knelt beside her and held her. "Okay, enough, let's say the Lord's Prayer together and hope that God is more kind then His priests."

# 9
## Pain

Smiljana stood in the doorway of the hospital room. Her eyes were tear-stained as she looked on at her sister and Milena. Stefan sat on a chair close to the bed. In one hand he held onto to Milena's hand and with the other he taped out an SMS message on his cell phone to Darko.

Irena was hooked-up to an IV, her face was pale bordering almost on a blue color. Milena had climbed awkwardly onto the bed. She deposited herself in a kneeling position and pulled her mother up into a leaning position resting her broken form against her chest. She kissed her mother on the cheek with her tears bathing her mother's face.

She prayed unashamedly out loud, "Daddy God, please, please let her live, let her have some joy, none of us deserve it, but I pray for her."

Stefan gently squeezed Milena's hand. He knew now he loved her and wanted to spend his life with her. She was so gentle and so kind. He wanted to protect her, love her, be friends with her and change the world with her.

Smiljana spoke, "Mili." Stefan had never heard Milena called this before. "Mili, I have got to tell you what I told Yanchi, you have to know." Milena gently removed her hand from Stefan's and reached out to Smiljana to come. She sat next to them on the bed and stroked Irena's hair. "I have to tell you something really shocking." Milena's large brown eyes looked on with compassion and understanding not realizing that in a few seconds her life would be altered forever. "Your mother is your mother but Yanchi is not your father."

In that moment the whole room seemed to go into a state of silent shock. Milena just looked at her auntie then at Stefan. "Your father is someone that you have never met. Your father is Yanchi's brother Radovan."

The state of shock continued as Milena just stared into the distance as if just for a moment trying to take it in. She could not speak. Smiljana continued. "I told Yanchi today, so you cannot go back there." Milena nodded and held her mother tightly. Then spoke to her in a whisper. "Oh Mama, this is why you have been so burdened, oh Mama, I love you so much."

Smiljana continued, "The Mujere, you call her Teta Nada, she knows and she and Radovan have been paying for the food and books for you all these years."

Milena held her mother closer and rocked her in her arms. Stefan leaned forward and held them both in his arms.

"Anyway, you cannot go back to the village, Yanchi will do something to you." Stefan spoke. "You can come and stay with my family until we sort things out, we have an extra room." "Let me go in the car, I can get down and back in a couple of hours. I will talk to my parents and then I will come back for you."

Smiljana spoke, "I have your bike, you can take it over to Teta Nada and I will stay here with Irena."

Stefan walked into the cold night air across the parking lot his mind was swimming with conflicting emotions. The thought of Milena suffering more made him determined that he would protect her and ultimately love her and marry her. As he closed the door to his car and turned the key he found his voice rising, "Oh Jesus, I love this girl, I love this girl."

The hospital room was now almost silent. Milena lay on the bed next to her mother gently stroking her head. Smiljana sat on a chair and rested her head close to them both. She spoke. "I think you should go over to Teta Nada now and wait there just in case Yanchi comes."

She leaned over and kissed her mother on the forehead and left the room. The nurse was just coming in and asked Milena to come outside the room. She spoke. "I know your mother is very ill, but she has improved and we think now that she is going to live." Milena thanked the nurse walked a little farther and leaned against the wall.

She could feel love, warmth and relief welling up inside of her. As she walked out into the cold night a flood of feelings swept over her. She was relieved beyond words her mother would now probably live. She felt confusion but joy that Yanchi was not her father. She felt deep love and affection for Stefan satisfied by that experience alone, knowing that he would never marry her but that she had a friend. She had someone she could focus feelings and love and affection upon. She looked up into the cold night sky. She could see her breath breaking into the cold. Then in a violent invasion into her reflections she found herself thrown to the ground with just the sight of a boot as it smashed into the side of her head. She was so stunned she could not speak. The trunk of Yanchi's car was opened and she could smell his fowl breath as he roughly picked her up and threw her inside. The sound of the slamming of the trunk and then the sound of her bike being run over by the car was her last memory as she slipped into unconsciousness.


Stefan sat with Darko and Marija in their flat. Darko tried to keep a calmness about him but the pain of heartbreak was something that he wanted Stefan to be kept from. "What is the

## Jasmina, Darko and Milena

prime principle in Social Work?" Stefan nodded and spoke. "I know, I know but this is different. It worked for Ivan and Jasmina."

Darko smiled knowingly and with compassion. "Okay, I knew that that was going to come, but anyway she's in danger now and we need to help, but I think it would be better if she stayed with Ivan and Jasmina anyway."

Stefan sighed in relief. "Thank you, thank you, I will go and get her and bring her here then we can decide what to do."

Radovan shook with emotion as he listened to Teta Nada explain that Irena had been taken to the hospital and may not live. Radovan spoke with a quivering voice but was clear in his intent. "Okay, I will come back and explain everything to my brother and to Milena." He hung up the phone and sat down quietly. He could feel his heart pounding for a moment he thought he could audibly hear it. He spoke to himself. "And so the day has finally come."

After driving yet again up the highway Stefan arrived at the Hospital. Smiljana told Stefan that Milena had gone to Teta Nada's. It was so late he decided to leave her to rest there, knowing that this dear woman would care for her overnight. He had decided to get a drink and something to eat just to give himself some space. He did not generally like the kavana's, as they all seemed to have an edge of darkness to their atmospheres. This one was no different.

There was a pool table sitting in the middle of the room with some young people playing. In one corner there was a pay-as-you-go music sound system that played the most dreadful music. Just to his left sitting at a table were some of the old boys sharing with each other the stories of their lives. It was from their conversation that he found his blood chilled. "I tell you it's true, tomorrow I'm going to get a woman, a gypsy woman as a slave its true, 300 Euros and she's mine to do with as I want." Stefan wanted to reach over and grab the old man by the throat. He continued as he lifted his glass. "To Yanchi, my father-in-law to be and to Milena my future wife and slave."

# 10

## The Deal

Milena sat still on the edge of the bed. The pain in the side of her head seemed to increase rather than diminish as the hours had dragged on. It was cold outside but the heat of the small wood stove caused a claustrophobic feel to the room. Yanchi stood leaning against the wall. Occasionally he would say something cruel.

Looking through the window Milena could see Tomislav waddling through the mud. His face was red and he looked out of breath as he walked. She had tried to bring her heart to peace but could not. Yanchi had made it so clear. If she did not marry this old man he would kill Irena. She fought with herself all night and finally came to the conclusion that her mother had suffered so much that she would have to sacrifice herself for her.

The door opened and her future husband walked through into the warm oppressive room. The foul smell that accompanied his entry gave her a feeling of sickness. She did not look up but rather stared at the floor, her mind reeling from all that was happening. She was still in a state of shock after learning that Yanchi was not her father. She felt as much relieved as she did confused. Tomislav sat down and tried to recover his breath. Yanchi poured him a drink and then lifted his glass. "To my son-in-law." He burst into the laughter as he said the words.

Tomislav laughed too as he coughed and wheezed. It was then that Milena saw his teeth that were yellow and green and caused her to feel as if she would vomit.

Her case was packed. Her precious box of books would stay

behind, she would have no time for reading Yanchi had told her. She had packed though her New Testament. She knew that to plead or beg would only degrade herself and would have no effect. She thought of Stefan. She had thought of him all through the night. She loved him but they could never marry. She was deformed. She had never used the kind of toilets that he had grown up with as being normal. He ate with a knife and fork and she only ever with a spoon. He slept in a clean bed with sheets, she would either lie on the floor or at the bottom of Yanchi and her mother's bed. She would always love him though and thank God for him. He would be the place she could focus her heart as she was being forced into the dreadful place with Tomislav. She would pray for Stefan and that would be where she would meet him in her spirit.

  Then there was God. The last weeks had seen her life change forever. She loved God now genuinely. Her precious New Testament had become alive to her and she lived within its pages, not in the fantasy of her imagination but in real meaning and purpose.

  Tomislav took out his wallet and drew 15 twenty Euro notes from it and placed them on the table. Then from the inside pocket of his jacket he took a piece of paper and placed it next to the money. He smiled to himself and then looked all over Milena's body. He took a pen and signed the paper. He slid the sheet of paper across the table and handed the pen to Yanchi.

  Radovan got off the bus and was greeted by Smiljana. He kissed her on both cheeks. She spoke. "It's been a long time Radovan but you look healthy." Radovan nodded and then spoke. "How are Irena and the little one?" "Little one, she is a woman, Irena will live but she is very ill. What are you doing here anyway?" Radovan turned to walk away from the bus and he put his hand on Smiljana's shoulder. "I've come to put things right. I need to explain everything

## Jasmina, Darko and Milena

to Yanchi, I have to confess to Irena, and I have to see my daughter and tell her everything."

Yanchi held the pen in his hand. He looked at Milena and smiled. The sense of revenge filled him with a genuine delight. He looked at Tomislav and smiled again. The 300 Euros represented a couple of really serious days of drinking but it was not the money he wanted it was the feeling of being in control. He reached out to sign the paper when suddenly the door flew open.

Stefan stood in the doorway. There was something both fresh and innocent about him yet at the same time an edge of the unpredictable. He looked at Milena with a pleading knowing look for her not to be afraid and then shouted at Yanchi. "Put the pen down!" Tomislav who was standing shouted himself. "Sign it, and sign it now!" Milena closed her eyes and tried to focus her heart on praying that something good would come of this madness.

Stefan quickly snatched the paper from Yanchi's hand before he could act. Yanchi sat down on a chair and took one of Tomislav's cigarettes from a packet on the table. He smiled as he lit and then drew from the tobacco. "We will just fill out another piece paper. You can keep that one as a souvenir for when Milena and her husband are kissing each other in delight."

Stefan looked deeply into Yanchi's eyes without blinking that created sense of unease in his heart. Stefan spoke with a quiet yet deliberate voice. " There are several ways we can do this, if you sign that paper and I leave without Milena, I will return again but this time I will bring hell with me."

Tomislav trying to get back into some kind of control spoke. "It's a business deal and it has nothing to do with you." Yanchi looked at Tomislav and then at Stefan. Again Tomislav spoke the same words. "It's a business deal and it has nothing to do with you."

Stefan ignored the words and took an envelope from his inside jacket pocket. He turned towards Milena and tried to cause her to be at peace with his look of love. She stood now gazing into Stefan's eyes, he was such a good man. Cold waves of fear yet excitement seemed to sweep all over her.

Stefan spoke, "Well if it's a business deal then maybe we can negotiate." Yanchi laughed. "Only partly business, I know you're going to offer more money, but it's not about the money. I have been deceived and now I'm going to have my revenge."

Stefan opened the envelope and then spoke. "This is a deed for a property I own, it's worth 60,000 Euros. I've been to the notary and signed it over to you. All you have to do is sign it and it is yours. If you do Milena is mine, and her books, and I will leave with her now and that is the end of the story."

Yanchi looked pale. Milena began to weep and Stefan walked over to her and placed his arm around her shoulder. Yanchi spoke almost in a gasp. "It is a trick, it has to be a trick, she's not worth 300 Euros but 60,000 Euros is crazy."

Tomislav interjected in an almost whining fashion. "You made a deal you cannot break your promise." Yanchi laughed. "Oh yes I can." He looked at Stefan in wonder. "You have a deal." He then signed the deed. Milena thought she would faint. Stefan gently lifted her into his arms and carried her slight almost weightless form through the door. He called to a young boy to get Milena's bag and box of books. For just a moment he stood in the fresh cold air and looked out over the village. Milena had her eyes closed and her face snuggled into his chest. The whole village stood in a line almost like a guard of honor as Stefan walked through their midst. Milena's almost childlike grip tightened.

She whispered, her eyes still closed. "I love you Stefan." Stefan gently put her down and then helped her into the car. The whole village surrounded them. Stefan took the bag and the box of books and put them in the back of the car. Suddenly and seemingly out of nowhere the same old lady who stood by the edge of the village when Irena was taken to the hospital in the ambulance came and stood by them. She was now ancient looking and withered. She shuddered for a moment that caused fear in the little children who were all around. Then in a gasping voice she spoke.

" The curse has been broken, I can feel it, this is something very powerful, very powerful." Stefan squeezed Milena's hand. " She has no idea how powerful the Blood of Jesus is to break any and every curse."

    He started to drive away and as often is the case in high tension situations he spoke in a way unrelated to the drama they were experiencing. "You know the first thing that I am going to make for you, a bookcase ."

# 11

## The Dark Imagination

Tomislav's room seemed darker than usual this morning. He had slept little after spending much of the night wrestling in his heart and mind concerning what he must do. His mind had become a mixture of religious symbols from his childhood and imaginations of being thought of as a nationalist hero. He stood in front of the mirror muttering to himself. He held a large felt marker in his hand then created a large letter "u" on the mirror in front of him. Then between the two awkward stems of the "u" he drew a cross.

He smiled as he took the photograph of his father and uncle Ante and then placed it in his jacket pocket. Yanchi had betrayed him. Yanchi was a gypsy. All gypsies are of bad blood and bad character. He knew that now and he had repented to the Blessed Virgin of his sins. His penance was to make right the betrayal that had been committed.

Yanchi had also blessed him by revealing that the young man that took his woman was a Serb. This information was not enough to redeem Yanchi but it would mean that his stay in purgatory would be cut short. He reached into the drawer and took out an old German Lugar pistol. He crossed himself and then took the bullets from a small box and placed them the chamber. He sat down on a chair next to a small table. He took a pen and wrote on a piece of paper. His words were confused but were short punctuated statements about doing the will the God and how he would soon be at The Hague with Gotovina and other men who loved their country's blood and were not afraid to do what was right.

## Jasmina, Darko and Milena

It was now time to leave. He crossed himself again and then stood in front of the mirror and made a salute. His wasted life would now be redeemed. He thanked the mother of God once more and then walked through the door into the street that was bathed in sunshine.

Irena lay in the hospital bed and was propped up with several pillows. There were small plants on the outside of the window in a long box that gave a splash of color to an otherwise bare and plain room. Milena sat next to her and occasionally lent across to kiss her.

Irena looked tired and defeated and yet had a deep glowing beauty that seemed to be surfacing from a place that it had been hidden for so long. Stefan came into the room and lent over to kiss his fiancée on the forehead. Milena's eyes shone with an almost iridescent glow that comes when such eyes are exposed to the bright light of morning. Her silk black hair created the context for her eyes to shine. There was something deep and beautiful about her far beyond the natural beauty of her face. It was as if some deep spiritual well of life had sprung open allowing the release of indescribable and indefinable goodness of spirit that had been made at peace with God.

Stefan reached up and gently squeezed Irena's hands, "You could be sisters." Irena smiled weakly and then began to cry, "I'm so sorry Milena, and I was so selfish." Milena gently reached out and put her finger on her mother's lips. "Hush now, if there is anything that you were guilty of, I have forgiven you, I cannot remember it anyway."

Stefan smiled and stroked Milena's hair, he loved her so much. The discovery of so many new things about her seemed to surface every time she spoke. The evening before as they drove away from the village she told him how much she had loved him and then had pleaded with him not to be angry with her. She had then gone on to say that she had wanted to wait until they were married before their lips met in a kiss. He had never thought about it before. She had read so many English novels from long ago and had suddenly made the connection with purity and love.

He had held her hand and made a promise to honor her. Stefan had leaned over again and kissed her forehead. "Well this is a big day, a very big day and I think it is going to be emotional, you're going to meet your father for the first time and you Irena will meet someone who loved you but wanted to do the right thing." Milena hunched her shoulders and shuddered with excitement, Irena closed her eyes and was silent. "Well if you are both ready then I will go and bring them in."

Yanchi realized that it was the happiest day of his life. He was rich. He was free from the burden of that cursed Milena and he had no interest in seeing Irena again. He had prostitutes for his needs and now he would have an endless source of money. He had decided that he would drive across to the Podravina and see his property. The envelope with the deed sat next to him on the front passenger's seat. As he drove through the mud of the village he felt like he had never felt before.

The cornfields were now empty. The wide and long horizon stretched out in a cold but bright landscape. The only disturbance to the joy of his day was the sight in front of him of the barriers coming down across the road at the railway crossing. He slowed down and then passed the three cars that were already stationary. He carefully edged his way around the first barrier and onto the railway track. Suddenly and it seemed instantly a train appeared.

He quickly accelerated but it was too late as the train was

upon him. The swift impact smashed into the driver's side and Yanchi could for a moment feel that cold steel of panic and fear run through his body. In an instant he was dead. The car pushed along the track with the petrol tank ripping open against the iron rails. There was a second's delay and then a burst of flames and then an explosion. Yanchi's charred body was thrust out onto the track with the contents of the car vaporizing in an instant.

Tomislav got off the bus and made his way to the hospital. He looked across at a block of flats and saw children playing in a small recreation area. He prayed as he walked past, "Mother of God it is for them that I do this, they must have a country to grow up in that is clean." The feel of his gun pressing against his chest gave him an intensified sense of destiny. 'Tomislav', he thought to himself, the very word itself represents strength and national pride. At The Hague they will learn to respect that name. And those Serb dogs in the other cells will fear it, oh yes they will fear it. They will not sleep easy knowing he was near.

Stefan walked back into the room; the expectation was almost palatable. He smiled and then stood aside as Irena's sister Smiljana and Radovan walked in. Radovan stopped immediately and stood and stared. Then in a faltering voice simply uttered, "Hello Irena." Stefan quickly stepped across to put his arm around Milena's shoulders. She was looking at her father for the first time and she was drinking deeply from the experience.

Radovan looked at her intensely. "The last time I saw you, you were a little baby, you are beautiful just like your mother." He leaned slightly to look at her ear. "But I can see you have my ear." Milena gently caressed her ear and spoke. "Yes, I know, Mama told me about it this morning."

Radovan wanted to reach out and hold both his daughter and her mother. He stood unable to move. "I have come to try and put things right. I am going to tell Yanchi everything, I sinned against him and you, Irena. I still love you now as much as I did then but I was wrong. I should have come sooner to rescue you but thought I could not because you were married to Yanchi. I am so sorry…" He could go on no longer and burst into tears. Smiljana put her hand on his shoulder. Irena wept like a child who took no thought about what the weeping appeared like. Milena reached both of her hands to her father as she spoke. "It is okay we can all forgive and be forgiven."

Before she had finished her sentence Tomislav had walked into the room holding gun in front of him. Radovan quickly rushed towards him but was immediately shot in the chest. The impact of the bullet hitting him both stopped him in his tracts and sent him in a twisting action to the floor. Tomislav raised the gun this time to Stefan and fired just as Milena threw herself in front of him. She was hit in the side and crumpled to the floor just as Stefan was taking the impact of a bullet fired at close range. As he fell his body turned and already a pool of blood had formed as he went face down to the floor. The screaming and the noise of the gunfire had brought an avalanche of hospital workers who quickly wrestled Tomislav to the ground.

For a moment there was silence as Radovan was in a hunched seated position against the wall trying to make his way to Irena. Stefan lay silent in a pool of blood with the bloodied form of Milena lying across his body.

# 12

## Saved By The Blood

The ceiling fan whirled above Stefan's bed. On either side of his bed were monitors measuring his vital signs. His face had a deep pale almost gray complexion. He was alone in the room other than two doctors who had been caring for the victims and cleaning up after the carnage.

The local media had come and gone quite quickly but the heavy weight TV, radio and newspaper reporters were soon to descend from Zagreb. Everyone knew the headlines were going to be something like 'GYPSIES AND SERBS BUTCHERED BY USTASHE'. All kinds of theories had begun to circulate. Dr. Zlatko Vidich, the older and senior doctor, had put it succinctly when he told his young partner Dr. Zoran Horvat, "You know how it goes, wherever there are two Croats there are three opinions." Dr. Horvat smiled partially to show respect for his older college but without agreeing directly with him.

Dr. Vidich had the reputation of being a renegade. He had worked as an army doctor in Vukovar and had seen everything it was possible to see in terms of human destruction. He had been though moved along to Chakovets rather than take a good position in Zagreb. The rumor was that he had argued constantly with the Generals and was known to be negative towards the nationalism that had swept the country after the war. Dr. Horvat looked at the monitors and then turned to Dr. Vidich. "We have used all the blood in reserve. It will take an hour before we can get any more. I don't think he can make it."

The nurse sat next to the bed where Milena lay. She was unconscious but from time to time stirred, the nurse checked her pulse and blood pressure. Everyone in the surgery was amazed at her strength and the way her vital signs had stood up. They had made jokes about Gypsies being made of special material.

Milena stirred then opened her eyes. She smiled at the nurse then spoke. "Where is Stefan? He was hurt I must go to him."

The nurse took a cool wet cloth and gently wiped her forehead. "You can see him soon but you have had a big shock to your body."

Milena was heavily sedated and started to drift in and out of consciousness. The nurse spoke to her again. "You are our miracle girl though, I asked the doctor if I could be the one to tell you." Milena smiled. "What is your name?" The nurse smiled and said "Dragica, Dragica Tesich." "Dragica, that is a lovely name, I am Milena."

The nurse smiled and found herself captivated by Melina's innocence. "Well Milena I have some lovely news for you. The doctors were taking the bullet out of your and they were able to correct your hip, it really was not that hard. You will be able to walk normally after you get better."

Milena started to shake all over just as she had when she read the story of Jesus healing the deformed woman. The medication had taken away any emotional restraint and she wept as a child. The nurse wiped her forehead and found herself swept into the emotion. Milena spoke through her tears, "I have to tell Stefan, I have to…" The emotional exertion plus the sedation took her from the conscious world to a peaceful place of dreamless sleep.

Dragica stood looking at her peaceful form and then shocked herself as she bent forward and kissed her forehead.

## Jasmina, Darko and Milena

Dr. Vidich was more tactile in his investigations and assessment than his partner. He touched Stefan's neck and under his armpits and then spoke. "We need blood now or he is going to die. You know the gypsy girl is stable I think we could use her blood to keep him going for a while, their blood types are the same."

Dr. Horvat had a look of horror on his face. "You can't be serious it would be illegal, you may kill them both, with all respect Sir, if anyone found out we would be ruined."

Dr. Vidich laughed and put his hand on his junior colleague's shoulder. "You are right, of course you are, I was just thinking out loud, we did it on the frontlines all the time. Actually I know gypsies and they are tough as you can get trust me, if Bird Flu comes through here we will all die but the gypsies will all survive."

Dr. Horvat sighed in relief just as his pager called him to another patient, he spoke as he left the room. "I will be about 30 minutes. We need to prepare this boy's parents for the reality that he is not going to make it. Can you call the priest for the last rights?"

Dr. Vidich nodded in agreement as the door closed. He quickly opened the door again and checked if his colleague had gone and then called for a nurse to come. "Bring Milena Orshus in here we're going to do a trans-human patch." The nurse obeyed without questioning and wheeled Milena into the room. She was unconscious but stable. She looked peaceful and had a warmth to her face despite being asleep.

"Put their arms together in a tunicae and then syringe her in a closed cath. I will do the same to him." As the equipment was set into place Milena started to stir. She spoke softly. "What are you doing?" Dr. Vidich swore under his breath. Then told the nurse to unhook Milena and take her back. It was then that Milena saw

# The Roma Chronicles

Stefan.

"Stefan, how is he? Please, please tell me the truth." The doctor leaned close to her. "Do you know him?" She smiled as she spoke with pride. "He is my fiancé." The doctor smiled almost in a wide grin. "Well, I want to give him some of your blood, as he is very, very ill." Milena reached out her hand and gripped the doctor's arm with the little strength she had. "Give him all my blood, he must live, it is more important that he lives then me." "You gypsies, sorry Roma, are so dramatic, I hope I can keep you both alive. Nurse, hook it up."

The unconventional transfusion took place as Milena and Stefan's arms were hooked together through a variety of innovative syringes. Milena started to drift again but spoke as she gently went to sleep. "It's just like Jesus, just like Jesus, He gave his blood to save my life, Stefan gave all he had to save me and now I give my blood to him."

Dr. Vidich hummed to himself as he worked. Shortly, the makeshift transfusion was dismantled and he instructed the nurse to leave Milena where she was for the moment. The door opened and Dr. Horvat walked in and spoke as he entered, "Any change?" He paused, saw Milena and then leant against the wall. "Please, Sir, tell me I have not seen a breach of protocols that will have me working in Knin Hospital for the rest of my life."

Dr. Vidich smiled, "Gracious, I would never, well anyway the kid is doing better, and if your people can get the plasma here we will save him." The nurse was still standing by the doctors with one hand resting on Milena's bed. "It is like a film, in the surgery today they corrected this girl's hip whilst cleaning out the gunshot wound and now this, this is just beautiful." Dr. Horvat nodded and walked across to his senior partner. "This never happened and you owe me, okay?" Dr. Vidich smiled and nodded. "You are learning the trade doctor, you will do well."

## Jasmina, Darko and Milena

Three days later Radovan sat in a wheel chair next to Irena's bed he was pale but feeling stronger. She was slowly recovering her strength. He held her hand and gently caressed her head with his other hand. "You need time to heal. Yanchi, as bad as he was, was your husband. I'm going to go back to my sister's but I'm going to come back very soon." Irena spoke through her tears. "Please don't leave me again, I need you now so much." Radovan squeezed her hand. "Okay, I will take you with me but we will not live together until we are married. I want you and I to find God like Milena and Stefan and Teta Nada. Irena kissed his hand and closed her eyes. "They are so clean, aren't they?" "Yes they are and I want us to be clean like them. I love you Irena, I always have, and I always will."

Darko and Maria sat by Stefan's bed. On the other side Milena sat in wheel chair. Darko reached into his pocket and pulled out an envelope. "The deed, oh the deed that created this American cowboy movie. I guess the original was destroyed but here is the copy. I've checked it all out and it is the same."

He looked across to Milena whose eyes were wide open. He spoke to her first in Bayash and then in Croatian. "Milena, Maria and I are the only parents that Stefan has. He is though our son and we love him as our own. You, little one, are the finest and most lovely woman that he could ever have for a wife and we are proud to have you in our family."
He looked at Maria and then smiled and spoke again.
" I have spent my life trying to escape Roma culture, but it just keeps coming around."

Maria stood up and walked around the bed and held Milena in her arms. Milena held Stefan's hand. "Jesus did heal me Stefan, didn't He?"
Stefan gently stroked her face and smiling through eyes filled with tears he spoke, " Yes he did, He really did."

# 13

## The Wedding

The group stood in a half circle facing the camera. At one end stood Milena and Stefan. She was wearing a long white, pure white, gown. She wore a white silk scarf that covered here hair at the top but allowed for two long braids to hang free and alive on either side of her shoulders. She held a delicate selection of wild flowers that Stefan had collected that very morning. He had said that she was so beautiful in the natural sense of the word that to bring flowers from a shop would be almost a sin.

Standing next to her was Lydia holding a bouquet of flowers, these ones had come from the shop. Next to her were Irena, Radovan and Smiljana. Standing next to Stefan were Darko and Marija, next to them Ivan and Jasmina.

Jasmina wore a green silk scarf similar to Milena and also allowed her hair the same freedom in two manicured braids.

Milena's faced glowed in a way that can only be experienced by seeing it and words leave the scene malpracticed in both beauty and depth.

The photographer took one more set of pictures and then announced that the selection of pictures was complete.

Stefan and Milena went into a side room were they would both change into more casual clothes to drive away in to their honeymoon.

Stefan drew Milena close to him and she nestled her face into the side of his neck. He whispered gently into her ear. " Before we go I want to pray for you." She snuggled even closer to him. She felt so safe and so full of joy. " Lord, there is no more precious woman on earth to me than this gift, my beloved Milena." He began to well up with emotion. " Lord, I want to make a covenant with you that my heart and body will belong to her and so will my eyes. Let me be a servant and a protector for her and may she know only security and peace in her life with me Lord."

He squeezed her close to him and she now looked into his eyes filled with love and devotion. Her lips reached out to his slowly and she closed her eyes.

Radovan and Irena sat on the bus close to each other. She held onto his arm as if to say that she would stay there. He leaned over and kissed her on the forehead. They both looked at the countryside as it rushed by them. " Radovan, do we have to come back here? Can we just start again somewhere else and have a completely new life together?"

He smiled. " Sure, we can, sure we can." She closed her eyes and leant on his shoulder and after a short time drifted into a warm and safe sleep.

Darko and Marija walked into the graveyard where his mother and sister were buried. They held hands and slowly made their way to end of the graveyard where the Roma section was. The tiny graves were neatly kept as he came regularly to tend them. He reached down and cleared away some weeds that had grown up. He turned and spoke to Marija. " How do you feel? Have you lost a son or gained a daughter? " She too reached out to the grave and cleared some long grass that had grown up around the sides.

" You know when he came to me, right at the beginning, I thought this is how I would earn my way to God because of all the pain and bitterness and hatred that was in me. When we all found

God, or rather when God found us, I knew it was not something I could do to earn my way to God but it was what Jesus had done. But today there is a part of me that actually feels complete, like I have found the way of joy, by loving someone more than myself."

Darko nodded and smiled. " I know that is how I felt when I found you, it is like I don't know where I end and you begin, you really do have my heart." Maria reached out and kissed him. " And you have mine, you have mine."

Teta Nada sat by the fire with Bela at her feet. She had a cup of hot chocolate, which she held cupped in her hands. " Well Bela, this was a happy day." Bela looked up and then lay her head down again and slept.
Tea Nada thought back to the day that Radovan had come and they had begun this long journey together.
" Lord Jesus, you are so good, so good, thank you for letting me see this, but now I am tired. I want to come home to heaven as soon as possible."
She chuckled to herself rubbed Bela with her foot and sipped her hot chocolate.

# 14
## To Forgive and Be Forgiven

Milena and Stefan sat on a rock that protruded out from the sea. Both dangled their feet into the waters. She had never seen the sea before. The sun was warm but still below the strength it would reach in a few more weeks. She could feel the warmth of the sun upon the back of her neck, which gave her a sensation that she had never experienced before. The water softly kissed their rock as its gentle waves lapped towards the shore. It seemed inconceivable that this gentle flow could turn into a powerful and destructive force. There was little noise other then the sea and the distant sound of the sea gulls. The water was absolutely pure. Milena could see the colorful little fish darting in and out between the small rocks. The stillness of nature and the quiet comfortable love of their marriage made the moments sublime, precious and healing.

Milena reached out her hand to Stefan and then spoke. "This is more beautiful than I could have imagined. So much more than anything that I have read about in my books. God has been so good to me to give me you as my husband." Stefan's heart seemed to melt as she spoke. He squeezed her hand and replied.

"But God has given you to me and it is your love that He has used to heal my own heart."

Milena smiled, "I know we are on our honeymoon but there is something that I sense that God wants us to do." Stefan smiled. "Anything, you want."

## Jasmina, Darko and Milena

The car pulled over the bridge and made its way onto the main road back towards Zagreb. They did not speak as they drove but were enveloped in the overwhelming sense that they were inwardly becoming one at every level of their lives.

The visitor's room was bare and empty. There was a cold impersonal feel to the atmosphere. Tomislav walked in looking a broken man. He did not seem to be disturbed to see them. He stood still and seemed to be looking past them. He was clean-shaven and dressed in clean prison overalls. He did not sit down at first but spoke in a soft almost vulnerable voice.

"Have you come to take me to The Hague?" Stefan looked on with compassion and then spoke. "No sir, we have not. We came to visit you, to talk with you. Please sit down."

Tomislav nodded and then obeyed meekly. He sat staring at the couple. He looked strange and uncomfortable when Milena reached out and touched his hand.

"We have come to tell you that we forgive you completely. We cannot influence the law but we release you. Everyone can forgive and be forgiven." The words were spoken so softly and the gentleness of Milena's face made them even more velvet-like and kind.

The authority and power in the innocence of the statement shook Tomislav. For a moment he was silent. He moved his head to one side as if he was being reprogrammed at some deep inward level. The dreams of dark glory, nationalism and playing backgammon with Gotovina in The Hague evaporated. He could not speak but had a strange and puzzled look upon his face. Stefan spoke. "You need help and we want to help you."

Tomislav looked down at the floor unable to gaze into the might of their innocence. He shuddered and then began to shake. At first no tears came forward to ease his suffering just a groaning almost whining sound. He gulped in air and then suddenly burst into a flood of tears. Between his weeping he gasped. "Jesus, Mary and Joseph these are children! Why did I do it? Why did I do it?" Milena wept with him and then reached out to squeeze his hand. "Mary and Joseph are in Heaven but Jesus is here, here in this room, Jesus can help you, forgive you." She spoke again. "Do you have anyone, any family or relatives?" He leaned forward and nodded with an agony that seemingly came from deep within his soul. "No, no one, no one."

Milena held Stefan's hand as the room fell silent and still. The impersonal space of the prison visiting room seemed to fill up with the warmth of love. "We will be your family if you let us and Jesus will be your Savior if you ask Him. When you were trying to buy me, Stefan gave everything he had to rescue me. Jesus gave everything he had to rescue us from sin. When Stefan was dying then the doctor gave him some of my blood. When we were dead in our hearts Jesus gave his blood to wash us from our sin."

Tomislav continued to shake and weep as Stefan and Milena stood up and quietly left the room.

*Jasmina, Darko and Milena*

# Conclusion

A few days after the accident Yanchi's ashes were buried in a graveyard with no marker. No one attended the burial and no one in the village knew where they were buried. Milena wept when she heard and continued to try and locate them so she could place a headstone and some flowers.

Nina the prostitute died of AIDS alone and unloved.

Almost exactly one year after the day that everyone still talked about as the 'crazy day', Radovan and Irena were married. They had a son and continue to live close to Milena and Stefan.

Lydia became a close friend of the couple. Her life was forever changed after the encounter with Milena. They met on several occasions and she came to find a faith in God and a whole new life as a young woman. She married and lives happily with her husband and family in Koprivnica.

Dr. Horvat and Dr. Vidic continued to work together with the younger doctor becoming the head of surgery at the hospital. He would often talk about the old days when Dr. Vidich did things his own way.

Darko and Maria moved into a small house near to Stefan's property. Every Wednesday and Sunday the two families spend the whole evening together.

*The Roma Chronicles*

Teta Nada died suddenly just 6 months after Stefan and Milena were married. She left to Milena in her will her whole library of books. Bela also now lives with Stefan and Milena.

Smiljana wanted to be married and have children but believed herself to be too old at 34 years of age to have either. Shortly after Irena and Radovan were married she………well that is in another book.

Nearly nine months after the wedding Tomislav was taken ill and was placed in the prison hospital. He was often living between the two worlds of reality and fantasy. For the last several months he had entered into a place of rest and peace in his soul. At Christmas Stefan and Milena had permission to bring him a Christmas dinner and pray with him and read the Bible. He then suffered a stroke. He died with Milena and Stefan at his side. He kept repeating the words, "Everyone can forgive and be forgiven."

*Jasmina, Darko and Milena*

## Final Word From The Author

This is obviously a fiction story but it is based upon true experiences that my wife Nancy and I have had in Europe over these last years. Central to my thinking is that forgiveness is both found and given in innocence. In fact, my whole view of life is that innocence has authority to change our lives when it is a tool in the hands of God. For many people today innocence has been lost.

The good news is that God can reclaim and rebuild our lives through the unique forgiveness that he gives. I would love to write to you and talk through these issues if this book has touched you.

You can write to me in English, Bayash, Croatian, Serbian or Hungarian. The best way is by email at: bob@bobhitching.com

*The Roma Chronicles* ───────

# Coming Soon From Spear Books and Media

# The Jesus Accounts

This thirty minute documentary attests to the historical accuracy and reliability of the New Testament Gospels. It demonstrates unequivocally that the oldest manuscripts of the Christian Gospels are completely consistent with the present day Bible.
It explains in detail how this consistency has resulted from the dedication of New Testament scribes and other guardians of Biblical integrity. They devoted their lives to the accurate preservation of the Gospel accounts and the other documents making up the New Testament – just as Jewish scribes did for the Old Testament.

For more information and purchase details go to:

# www.TheJesusAccounts.tv

Spear Books
& Media

Printed in the United Kingdom by
Lightning Source UK Ltd., Milton Keynes
141904UK00001B/2/P